The Banks Sisters 2

The Banks Sisters 2

Nikki Turner

www.urbanbooks.net

Urban Books, LLC
97 N18th Street
Wyandanch, NY 11798

ISBN 13: 978-1-62286-957-2
ISBN 10: 1-62286-957-5

First Trade Paperback Printing March 2016
Printed in the United States of America

10 9 8 7 6 5 4 3 2 1

Distributed by Kensington Publishing Corp.
Submit orders to:
Customer Service
400 Hahn Road
Westminster, MD 21157-4627
Phone: 1-800-733-3000
Fax: 1-800-659-2436

The Banks Sisters 2

Nikki Turner

CHAPTER ONE

Today was better than yesterday. Tomorrow will be better than right here, right now. But as it stood at this precise moment, life was what it was. And it was a damn good day to be on the Richmond Police Force. Things were finally looking up for Detective Dugan and his dedicated team of hardworking men. They'd been praying for clues that might point them in the general direction of any and all assailants that were running amuck in their fair city. Not knowing if they had a bloodthirsty serial bank robber on their hands or just some daredevil copycats, the stakes were high. All the officers' jobs, raises, and promotions were in serious jeopardy as the mayor demanded results. The wall safe of the now-deceased Ghostman, discovered behind a picture, had finally been cracked wide open by an expert on loan from the next county. The safe's contents had been logged in and were ready to be inspected by a forensic team. A huge stack of assorted currency; several quick claim deeds to homes located in known drug zones; a small spiral notebook; a Breitling watch; and an android smartphone were discovered resting inside next to a gang of snapshots of seminude strippers.

Already designating their victim as one of the perpetrators in the bank robbery committed earlier in the day, Detective Chase Dugan beamed with pride. Not only did they have the masks used in the crime, but a bag containing some of the marked bills. Detective Dugan's desire now was to try to link this crime with the blood fest robbery-turned-homicide earlier in the week at the same branch. "Okay, everyone, take your time on this crime scene. We don't need any mistakes or mishaps. We have damn near every news agency within a hundred-mile radius camped right outside this front door lurking, hoping for a minor or major screwup." With that being said, the overly excited officer of the law looked down at his watch. A far cry in cost in comparison to the one found in the dead man's safe, Chase still felt like he was rich in other ways. Placing a call to the female he prayed would one day be his lady, the smitten detective was elated to share his good news.

"Yes, hello," Simone answered trying to keep her voice level and normal when every part of her was quaking with fear. Her sinner soul was terrified about what was seconds away from being said.

"Yes, Ms. Banks?" Detective Dugan spoke into the phone using a formal greeting instead of the playful one he'd used earlier in the day.

Simone's face registered her worry. "Detective?" she responded fighting to keep her emotions from overpowering her words. She prayed he couldn't easily hear the nervous and guilt sentiments she was experiencing.

"Oh my God! You will never guess how things unfolded shortly after you left."

"Really, how?" Simone asked, scared of his response. She hoped for the best, yet prepared herself for the worst.

"Well, we found him," he fought from shouting out in total elation and jumping for joy. "We got his ass, Simone! We got him!"

"You found who?" she braced herself continuing to playing the dumb role as not to incriminate herself or her sisters just in case Ghostman turned out to be a ho-ass buster and ratted out everyone he could think of.

"We located the guy. The one who hit the bank this afternoon; that's who," the detective laughed with satisfaction in his pitch. "Now we have yet to identify his accomplices, but it's definitely him. He's one of the main guys. He's probably the damn mastermind."

"Really? You think so? How can you tell it was him? Are you serious?"

"Yes, Simone, really, I'm serious as two heart attacks. I think this case is about to be a wrap real soon. Hell, we already have recovered some of the money along with the masks. That's how we know it was him."

"Oh, wow. Did you arrest him? Is he in jail?" The questions started coming one after one. Simone glanced over in the passenger's seat at Bunny praying her new beau would say yes.

"Unfortunately, no," the hardworking detective responded with utter regret. "He's not under arrest. Well, not really."

"Huh? Why not, baby? You said you guys had some of the stolen money and them crazy masks they were wearing, right?" Simone shook her head at her sister, then shrugged her shoulders. Knowing the police caught Ghostman red-handed with all the evidence Bunny had cleverly planted and he still wasn't behind bars was a mystery Simone needed for Chase to solve. "Please tell me why that animal isn't locked up. He and those evil men he runs with need to be in cages."

"Because things didn't work out like that. See, Simone, unfortunately, there was an altercation. Things went real bad real quick once we gained entry. The dude wanted to go for bad; all renegade style. The perp got shot after trying his luck with my men."

"Oh my God! Are you okay?" She showed her genuine concern for his overall safety and well-being.

"Yes, Simone, I'm fine. Thanks for your thoughts. I appreciate it. Matter of fact, you don't know how much it means to me."

"Of course, baby. You're always in my prayers as of lately. But I do just wish that madman was alive so he could tell you who the rest of those reckless monsters are that terrorized us down at the bank."

"Me too, Simone. I wish he was alive so we could have interrogated him about other stuff we think he's involved in. But you're right. He could have led us to the others in on the robbery with him. Now, unless we catch another break in the case, the other crooks can consider his death as a gift from the good man above."

"That's great, Chase, any way it went." Simone acted as if he'd single-handedly brought down the Taliban as she quietly giggled to her sister. "That's a huge relief you got that animal off the street, even if he is dead. Him and his friends were horrible. I hope one day you catch them all before they stick a gun in someone else's face. I'm still having nightmares about both robberies."

"I know, but at least you can sleep well, knowing one of them clowns is out of the picture for good." Chase tried not to smile too much as several of the reporters rushed in his direction. "Look, Simone, I have to go right now, and I need to reschedule our date for tonight, if that's okay with you."

Celebrating in her mind over what he'd just said about Ghostman, Simone happily agreed. "No problem at all. I understand. I'm just gonna go grab some Chinese food with my sister and relax for the evening. Call me later if you find the time. I miss you and can't wait to spend some time with you."

"Aww, that's so sweet of you to say. I miss you too. And for you, I'll make time." The detective placed his cell back on his hip, ready to answer the reporters' multitude of questions.

Simone hung up the phone, relieved that their plan worked, and to top it off, Ghostman was dead. He couldn't be interrogated or forced to snitch on anyone. There was nothing but thanks that they were in the clear.

CHAPTER TWO

"Well . . . well . . . What do we have here? Now you know good and well, either y'all can do that fed time waiting on y'all or run me some of that dough. As a matter of fact, y'all can run me *all* that!" Lenny pulled out a gun and stood guard as Deidra went for the cash. "Didn't Me-Ma teach y'all little hoes . . . easy come, easy go? Stupid asses!"

"Oh, hell, naw, this can't be happening," Bunny angrily blurted out shaking her head in denial. "Not your ass of all people! What the fuck are you doing here?"

"Oh, hell, yes, daughter of mine. This must be my lucky day." Deidra did a little praise dance waving her arms and hands around in the air as if she had the Holy Ghost tucked in her back pocket. "I asked the great hustle gods for a blessing, and here the fuck it is! Just like that . . . It was done!"

"What in the hell you talking about?" Bunny fumed, ready to kick some ass and take names later.

"I mean, damn, we came here to chin check that no good shepherd for Satan whenever he shows up for stealing my inheritance, and *bam!* Instead, we hit the jackpot! Hell, yeah!"

Bunny's impromptu champagne and Chinese food celebration came to a screeching halt, as it did for her three siblings. Smashing her glass down onto the rectangular-shaped kitchen table, Bunny was ready for war and anything that came with it. Still very much in mourning over the untimely death of the love of her life, Spoe, any bitch could get the business if they tried crossing her path—her no-good mother included. "Get the fuck on, lady, before I get pissed. If you think me and my sisters just gonna give you the money we risked our lives and freedom for just like that, you're more twisted in the head than I thought! You straight fucking nuts!"

"I'll be all that and more, but me and Lenny gonna get our share—period!"

"You think so, huh?"

"Yeah, I do. So like I said, run it. Don't keep us waiting! We got shit to do!"

"Seriously? You can't be!" Bunny's resentment grew, and her tolerance level plummeted to zero. She was ready to snap and pop any second.

"Yes, seriously! What part of 'run me all this bread' don't you and the rest of these misfits understand? I know all of y'all can understand English!" Deidra, although she called the streets her home, usually kept herself together. But today, she looked different. Maybe the death of Me-Ma had affected her far worse than she'd let on; but that still was no excuse or ghetto pass on strong-arming the next person's shit.

Coldly staring her mother in the eyes, years of bottled up emotions poured out. Without an ounce of fear for the weapon being held on them, contempt filled Bunny's tone after snatching the brown bag from her mother's greedy clutches. "You and this scheming leech you been laying up with got the game all messed up. You might have stolen Me-Ma's money and got over, but trust, this ain't what you want—gun or not. Not today, bitch. Matter of fact, not *no* day!"

"Watch your damn mouth when you speaking to me, Ms. Thang. I'm still your mother, and make no mistake—I'll still kick your uppity ass with the quickness."

Deidra tried to boss up, but her threat fell on four sets of deaf ears.

"My mother? Come on now, Deidra, with all that." Bunny called her by her first name, further proving she had no reverence for the belligerent creature that'd given her birth.

"Yeah, little girl; your damn mother, like I said to all four of you no-good bastards. Run me my shit! Now!"

"You know you ain't been our mother since the day we escaped from that polluted womb of yours. You ain't been a mother to any of us! Never-fucking-ever."

Deidra was unmoved by her child's insults. Always ready to defend her selfish lifestyle, she gladly returned the favor twofold. "I'm sorry, baby girl, but shouldn't you be somewhere mourning that dead stickup boyfriend of yours, or is one of them other hot-tail bitches he probably ran with doing that? You can say what you want about my man being a leech, but at least he's alive!" she laughed coldly.

Simone, usually the voice of reason, interjected, putting her two cents on the floor before her sister became totally untamed. They had gotten away with robbing the bank, saving Bunny from Ghostman's wrath, and getting him blamed for the crime. Plus the idiot got himself killed, to boot. Today had been a day full of wins, and Simone wasn't going to allow Deidra to break that streak. "Look, why are you here anyway, Momma? Who let you in? And why you just gonna let this man point that thing at us like we some strangers off the street and not your own flesh and blood?"

"First of all, Simone, I don't need any one of you ungrateful little hood rats to let me into my damn mother's house. Just because your daddy came up on the dirt he was peddling and raised you with a silver spoon in your mouth don't mean you can run it any way you want to."

"Oh my God!" Simone fell back, sucking her teeth.

"Yeah, maybe Me-Ma let y'all act all crazy and run off at the mouth, but me? I ain't the one. Shidddd, I'll knock all your heads off like it ain't nothing." Deidra couldn't believe her ears and what she was hearing. Taking a few steps backward, the unfit parent laughed. "If y'all didn't get the memo years ago, I'm grown and come and go as I please around here. Secondly, if you three girls and whatever the fuck you is today," she callously motioned to Ginger as if he were a freak of nature, "don't like what I'm saying, gather my money up and me and my man will be on our merry-fucking-way without anyone getting hurt. Or do y'all want me to call the police? Maybe that nosy, fine-ass cop you talking to Simone . . . How about that? So now that I've made myself once again clear, run me my shit!"

"Say *what?*" Simone paused, wondering how Deidra knew she was dating a policeman.

"That's right, you little neighborhood snitch bitch. I know everything. The streets talking loud, and you and all these rats in heels' names are ringing. Now should I call the police or what?" Deidra smirked, winking her eye at Simone.

"The police?" Tallhya interrupted, swallowing a huge lump in her throat.

"Yes, baby, I said it; the damn police. Didn't you hear me?"

"Are you serious?" Tallhya asked.

"Yes, I'm serious as two heart attacks. Either you girls can cut me and my man in or cut it out. Y'all already let that high-steppin' preacher steal this house and all my mother's freaking money."

"Let . . . ?" Bunny, fed up, was once again on Deidra's no-good ass. "We ain't let his crooked ass do jack shit. And since he did con Me-Ma, that means you just gonna gank our come up? Where they do that at? You're a real piece of work—rotten to the core. For sure."

Deidra sneered, glancing up at the wall clock. She'd heard just about enough of jaw jacking from her off-spring that she was willing to endure. Done taunting her four children-now-turned-bank-robbers, she was ready to collect what she felt was due to her and bounce. "Well, as far as I see, y'all come up is now *my* come up!" Feeling as if she had the heart of a lion, she brazenly brushed past a noticeably quiet Ginger. Under the twitching eye of Lenny, she bent down attempting to swoop up a handful of unmarked hundred-dollar bills scattered throughout the kitchen floor.

"Hold up, now." Simone roughly grabbed her mother by the forearm, snatching her backward. "Like Bunny said, we not just gonna let you take what's ours. That's not what's gonna go down. We ain't little kids no more—remember that."

Deidra was in no mood to be denied. Me-Ma had already slapped her in the face by leaving the church and Pastor Street the inheritance she felt was hers. Now her kids didn't want to share their come uppings. "Okay, bitches, I'm done playing with y'all. Lenny," she hissed with malice, not being able to bully them as usual with her words, "shoot the first one of these wannabe street-tough hood rats that puts their hands on me! Send them on their way to see Me-Ma." Deidra's voice got louder with each passing word. "Maybe they can ask her dumb ass why she fucked us all over! Shiddd . . . I mean, was that sissy preacher giving her old ass that rainbow dick or what!" she laughed.

That over-the-top announcement brought a momentary hush across the kitchen. With his palms sweating and the strong smell of cheap wine seeping from his pores, Lenny tried to look as ruthless as possible. Trembling from needing a drink, he fought to hold it together. Just as money hungry as his female companion, the low-life parasite hoped to live large off the enormous amount of revenue he was seeing as well.

"Look, you soulless trick! Have you lost your fucking mind altogether? Do those streets you live in got you that confused that you think you can march up in here making demands and threats like we ain't about nothing? And to top it off, disrespect Me-Ma's good name?" Simone fearlessly stepped front and center. Looking at Deidra like the gutter filth she was, she made it perfectly clear what exactly was and was not going to happen. "You and this fool are out of control, that much is clear, but you're going too far thinking shit will be that easy."

"What you say?" Deidra barked, feeling like she had the upper hand *and* the cops on speed dial.

"You heard me. Y'all clowns going too far, especially *you!*" Without warning or caution, Simone ran up on an obviously nervous Lenny. Now, almost nose to nose, she unloaded her fury and disdain for the stunt he was dumbly taking part of. "You coming up in my grand-mother's house pointing guns at people like you some sort of hit man or something; like you so damn gangster with it. Riding with my mother gonna get you killed one day, and today might be that day. If we had the balls to get this money, just imagine what the fuck we willing to do to keep it. You don't want this nigga. I swear you don't!"

Once again, the room grew eerily silent as Lenny's eyes bucked twice in size. He, like the others in the room, didn't know what to say. Tallhya buried her face in her hands, while Bunny's jaw dropped wide open. Ginger, who was playing the background up until this point, finally spoke up. Not wanting his sister to get killed trying to protect them or the stolen money, he looked at his mother, who was so desperate to get, wanting her to stop this madness. "Oh my God, Momma! Damn! Is this what you want? Is money so important that you want Simone or one of us dead to get it?"

With tensions running high, they all waited for a response from Deidra, but received none. Ginger had no more words for his conniving mother. She'd used him and his credit card scams constantly, without any remorse if he got arrested; so be it. Not even bothering to put a single penny on his books, Ginger knew what she was doing now there was no coming back from. Me-Ma was dead and gone, and as far as he was concerned, from this point on, Deidra was as well.

"Ginger, I done told you a million times to stop counting on Momma to change. She wasn't about shit when we was growing up and damn straight about shit now. But I got something for that ass . . . something real serious." Simone's feet were firmly planted where she stood. Still up in Lenny's face, she didn't blink or miss a beat. "Bunny, you and Ginger pick up that money off the floor and put it back in the bags!"

"Hold up, Simone." Bunny raised her eyebrow in protest.

"Naw, sis, I got this; just get the money!"

"Now you talking like you got some damn sense." Deidra, shiftless in her intentions, finally spoke. "Run me my bread; every damn penny!"

Allowing the over-the-top garbage her mother was yacking about to roll off her back, Simone continued telling her siblings what to do. "Bunny, y'all just get all the cash together that's on the floor. And, Tallhya, why don't you go make sure the front door is locked and come right back. Me and Mr. Gun-Toting Lenny right here got some unfinished business to handle."

Despite objections from Me-Ma, Deidra lived her life in the streets since she was a young teen. Seasoned to the game, she knew if you were trying to pull a stunt, run a scam, or plot on a scheme, you needed to be in and out as soon as possible. She knew the more time you spent living in the eye of the storm, the more chances your shit could fall apart. Unfortunately, her bank-robbing daughters knew the same thing; especially Simone. Knowing her mother was capable of snitching to the police if she didn't get her way, Simone knew she had to make a move to make that impossible. Although there was a strong possibility she could have cancer, she'd much rather fight that deadly beast disease than face a judge and whatever part of her life that was left on the earth locked up behind bars. Once again, thanks to her father giving her advance knowledge of firearms, Simone could easily see the once-powerful machine gun her mother's boyfriend-wannabe-henchman was holding was inoperable. The old relic may have been intimidating to some; however, Simone had been through too much over the past few weeks to be scared by a "dummy gun." She'd let her once-beloved mother have her say, but it was time to turn the tables.

"I don't know what you trying to say or do, but my man ain't gonna have no dealings with you whatsoever unless you thinking about putting ya hands on me!"

Simone's voice remained the same as she informed her mother what was to come next. "Believe me, for real—for real—not one of us want to touch you; at least not yet. But this motherfucker right here," she pointed her finger in Lenny's nervous face, "he about to see what it feels like to have a *real* Banks sister on his ass! I'm done being nice." Using both hands, she suddenly shoved Lenny's small wiry frame into the side of the refrigerator. Not scared of him pulling the trigger on the faulty weapon he was holding, Simone snatched it out of his sweaty hands before he knew what had taken place.

"Holding this old shit that don't even fire no more! I told you my mother was gonna get you hurt out in these streets! If she don't give a fuck about her own kids, you think she give a shit about you getting thrown under the bus? Stupid-ass motherfucker!"

Seizing the opportunity, Ginger stepped in, transforming into Gene in a matter of seconds. Delivering blow after blow closed-fist punches to the older man's face and chest area, Ginger broke two of her perfectly manicured nails off into Lenny's rib cage. Practically stomping the cheap wine out of Lenny's skin, Tallhya joined in the free-for-all melee as Bunny collared their mother up.

"Let me go, bitch! Let me the fuck go!"

"Naw, Deidra. You wanted to be here at Me-Ma's house so bad like you running thangs . . . well, welcome your black ass home." Bunny wrapped one hand up in Deidra's T-shirt collar and the other around her neck. She'd been waiting a lifetime to show and tell her mother how she truly felt, and today was as perfect a time as any. Unlike her partner in crime Lenny, Deidra tried to buck but was immediately shut down by Bunny's hands tightening around her throat. "You got some random-ass Negro in here pointing a gun at us? Talking like shit is easy, like thangs ain't hard enough on us! You ain't coming up on shit, bitch!"

Deidra struggled to speak as her mouth grew increasingly dry. "I swear to God if you don't let me go, you gonna regret it!"

"What, Momma?" Tallhya growled from across the room after seeing yet another kick into Lenny's bleeding mouth. "What you gonna do to us that you ain't already did? Abandon us? Lie to us? Cheat us out of our birthday gifts from other family members? Berate us and everything we try to do? What's left, Momma? Huh? What's left? You wanna go dig up Me-Ma's body so you can spit in her face? You foul! I hope Bunny chokes the life outta your ass!"

After making sure Lenny was unable to stand on his own, Ginger, using the manly strength he was born with, dragged him over to the basement door as instructed by Simone. Having no remorse for the beating the fool, Ginger let his battered, bruised body fall recklessly down the old wooded stairs. After hearing the distinct sound of him reaching the bottom, they each paused. Snatching a butcher knife out of the drawer, Simone knew her two sisters had Deidra covered. Holding the shiny blade up to her face, she made sure it was razor sharp. Tilting her head to the side, the nice-sister-now-turned-bad signaled for Ginger to follow her into the basement.

CHAPTER THREE

As much as she wanted to, Bunny loosened her grip, not wanting to actually kill her own mother. As Deidra fought off the disorientation of being close to death, Tallhya closed her eyes, trying relentlessly to not have one of her panic attacks. Fanning her hand in front her face in an attempt to get some added air flow, she started crying out for Walter's cheating self. Bunny grabbed a sales paper off the table and started waving it in Tallhya's face, begging her to calm down and take deep breaths.

"You bitches gonna pay for treating me like this. And them motherfuckers better not hurt my man anymore! Lenny! Lenny!" The mother of four shouted toward the basement door. "Hold on, love, I'm coming!"

"Shut your mouth! For once, shut your mother-fucking ratchet-ass mouth. Don't you see your child is going through something right now, and you calling out for some man?" Bunny frowned at Deidra, who was still down on the floor. "I promise it should've been you and not Me-Ma in that casket! A million of you ain't worth half of the woman she was."

Deidra had not an ounce of compassion for her children and their various troubles. Matter of fact, since they were treating her like what she felt was garbage, she decided to add more heart wrenching fuel to the fire. "Wow, Bunny, tell me how you really feel." She rubbed her sore neck as she spit more venom. "And, Tallhya, I don't know why you crying out for that no-good husband of yours while y'all talking about me running behind some man. I had a taste of that young, curved, uncircumcised dick a few months back. Yeah, when I caught him out at the club with that bisexual dead baby momma of his; showboating hard. I figured with the courtesy of you."

"What?" Puzzled, Tallhya's mouth went dry, as if she was hearing wrong.

"Yup, baby girl, we all partied together off your money and freaked until daybreak." Deidra had no shame exposing a few more hurtful truths. "I mean, the dick wasn't all bad, but it sure ain't worth clowning over. Hell, you might wanna look his baby moms up and let her eat your pussy. She sho' got better skills than Walter do!" A smile spread across her face. She knew exactly what she was doing—throwing rocks at a glass house.

Stunned at what she'd just heard, Tallhya's anxiety level increased as did her anger. It was bad enough her supposed loyal husband had an illegitimate baby with some tramp. And even worse, he'd admittedly stolen her lottery winnings. But now the bum allegedly had sex with her own mother, of all people. If what disgusting acts Deidra claimed were indeed true, that thought alone was more than the average strong-minded person could stand. Tallhya was fragile. Since being served divorce papers, the immediate family knew she wasn't in the mental state to endure any further emotional blows and tried to shield her from as much unwarranted bullshit as possible. Strangely, helping her siblings rob the bank earlier was some twisted sort of empowerment for her. Tallhya was actually feeling good about herself. It was hard, but she was willing to accept the reality she and Walter were over. Now, Deidra had the nerve to show up and drop this cruel bombshell. Divorcing the backstabbing creep was hard enough, but this betrayal was adding insult to injury.

"You know you the damn devil, don't you?" Bunny fumed, knowing her sister had to be devastated.

"You just better be lucky I ain't get a hold of that fine-ass Spoe. I would've really given his dead stickup ass a run for his money—guaranteed."

Slowly easing to the other side of the kitchen, Tallhya oozed with resentment. Her legs were numb. Her broken heart raced as she saw red. Pulling the oven door down, she kept her eyes focused on Deidra who was now preoccupied once again taunting Bunny's recent tragic loss of Spoe. Her mother had to pay for her sins. The injured emotions daughter saw no other way to make things right. Reaching her hand inside the oven, Tallhya removed one of her grandmother's favorite black cast-iron skillets she'd cook freshwater corn bread in. Raising it high over her head, her fingers tightened. The mentally distraught female's taste for revenge increased. Wanting to silence any more spellbinding revelations, Tallhya brought the heavy cookware crashing down onto the side of her mother's evil face. Hearing the certain sound of her jawbone crack, coupled with Deidra's agonizing pleas for mercy, Tallhya felt vindicated after the verbal tirade she'd just suffered at the hands of her wicked-minded mother. Dropping the skillet to the floor, Tallhya didn't say a word. She just stood there; frozen in some sort of a trance.

"Sis," Bunny loudly whispered, attempting to get Tallhya to snap out of it. After a few seconds, she called out to her sister once more, this time shaking her shoulder. Receiving no response, Bunny had no choice but to leave her standing zombied out in the middle of the kitchen floor. She'd have to deal with Tallhya and this episode later.

With blood leaking out Deidra's mouth and nose, and her face expanding twice its normal size, Bunny knew she had to get her down in the basement with her cohort Lenny as soon as possible. As Deidra squirmed around on the floor getting louder, Bunny didn't want any nosy neighbors or members from Me-Ma's congregation to show up unannounced. It'd certainly not be a good look if they discovered what atrocities were taking place in their beloved matriarch's home.

Quickly retrieving a damp dish towel by the sink, Bunny stuffed it into Deidra's mouth, warning her to shut the fuck up or risk far worse pain. Easily telling her mother's jaw was indeed broken, she was able to jam more of the cloth inside than would be normally possible. Leaning over, she grabbed one of Deidra's feet. Bunny wished she could order a now-bewildered Tallhya to lift the other, but knew at this point she was on her own. Dragging their still-feisty mom across the kitchen floor, Bunny opened the basement door. Yelling for Simone and Ginger to get out of the way, Bunny gave Deidra the same fate as Lenny: a trip down the wooden stairs, face-first.

Propped up against a cardboard box of Christmas tree decorations, Lenny was motionless. The inch-long gash on his head, courtesy of the fall, continued to spew blood at a rapid pace. Having broken several teeth when his mouth slammed down onto the concrete floor, Lenny's lips were split open as well. Stepping on the small sharp pieces of his yellow, plaque-stained dental, Simone was in total survival mode as she inhaled the stale dampness of the basement. Her mother's flavor of the month had the nerve to not only be in cahoots with her, but hold them at gunpoint as well. For that, justice would be swift. The beat down he got and the free trip down a flight of stairs was only a small bit of punishment. With the aid of a few old extension cords, she tightly tied his arms. Having cut up a few bedsheets that were hanging on the clothesline, Simone instructed Ginger to wrap the cloth around their nemesis's head so he wouldn't leak his germ-infested fluids all over the place.

"What we gonna do with him, girl?" Ginger was eager to follow her sister's lead. She'd masterminded them getting away with robbing the bank, so she'd earned the right to call the shots.

"We gonna do what we have to do; to him and Momma—*that's* what!" Simone showed no weakness glancing toward the top of the stairs as they heard a small bit of commotion. "We risked everything to get that money up there, and this ignorant fool and Momma ain't gonna take it—let alone get us knocked. I ain't trying to go to jail no time soon. Is you?"

"Hell, fuck, naw! Whatever you say, I'm down. I'm rolling with you." Getting incarcerated for armed robbery was not on her to-do list. Ginger had plans of going on a few elaborate shopping sprees and updating her vehicle. Her share of the money was going to enable her to live life to the fullest . . . drama free. Unlike her sisters, Ginger had absolutely no man problems or health issues at hand. Bunny was mourning Spoe's sudden demise. Tallhya was getting divorced from Walter's conniving ass, and Simone was falling in love with Detective Dugan, and unbeknownst to anyone, possibly had cancer. The illegal revenue was a much-needed distraction for them, and Deidra and Lenny would not become glitches in the system. Just as Simone and Ginger ensured Lenny couldn't break free from his makeshift restraints, the top door opened. Seconds later, Deidra, unceremoniously, made her way down the stairs to join her man.

Moving out of the way just in the nick of time, Simone dodged her mother's body that haphazardly flew down the stairs. Seeing it hit the floor, her limbs flung around like an old rag doll Me-Ma had sitting in the corner of the living room for decoration.

"Damn, girl! What in the hell happened to her head and face?" Simone's concern was short-lived when Bunny filled her in on what she'd said to Tallhya pertaining to Walter. Having had enough of her mother's evil spirit and everything that came with it, Simone had Ginger tie a still-dish-rag-gagged Deidra up with the remaining part of the shredded sheet they'd used on Lenny's head wounds.

"Okay, y'all," she announced seeing both of their problems were temporarily put on hold, "these assholes ain't calling the damn police on anybody no time soon, let alone spending any of our money. Now, let's go back upstairs and check on Tallhya."

CHAPTER FOUR

It was the crack of dawn. Detective Dugan had been up all night pressing the forensics team on any reports of additional evidence that could link others to the high-profile bank robbery. After making a positive identification of Ghostman aka Marky Amadeo, he knew this case was about to take him in several different directions all at one time. The deceased was not only involved in robbing banks but was implicated in over a dozen drug-related homicides, to boot. Ghostman was a well-known and connected Italian criminal in the underground world of the city of Richmond. When word spread of his sudden demise, Detective Dugan got call after call from his paid informants, giving him an update on what the streets were saying. While most believed a rival bloodthirsty drug gang originating from New York, the Bloody Lions Posse run by the infamous dread named Dino, had set him up, others rumored it was one of the many strippers he ran with. Maybe even the one whose name the condo was listed in. Wherever the complicated case might take him, a connection with Simone and her family never once crossed his mind.

"Thanks for putting a rush on the items. You know the FBI and the ATF are waiting for us to drop the ball." He stretched and yawned, trying his best to fight sleep.

"No problem, Chase. I got your back." One of the guys from the forensics department handed him several huge manila-colored envelopes. "And just so you know, we got some partial prints of someone other than our deceased gunman. We're trying to see if we can get a hit through the computers."

"Oh yeah?" He felt more optimistic about not needing the FBI or the ATF's assistance to solve the multiple cases. . . . If he'd only known the key factors to closing all the cases were just a phone call away to Simone.

"Yeah, man. I'll keep you posted. I'm on it. The chief is on my back too."

Having received the discovered android cell phone back from the forensics team, Detective Dugan studied each picture in the gallery, realizing none of the photos belonged to Ghostman. Without hesitation, he knew he'd seen the face in most of the pictures recently on the evening news. It became quickly apparent the cell phone seized from the wall safe belonged to the young man whose body was washed up along the bank of the James River, a well-known dumping ground drug dealers used to dispose of bodies. The detective remembered the man shot in the chest before he was tossed in the murky water's name was Tariq something or another. He, along with a few more bodies, was fished out the latter part of the previous week. After getting in touch with the homicide detective handling that particular case, the weary Chase started the long, grueling task of going through the extensive list of names and numbers in the contact list. Logging in the amount, dates, and times the owner called the most frequent numbers, he tried to find a pattern. After then carefully studying the iPhone Ghostman had on his hip when he was killed, and comparing the two, he felt like he might have been making some sort of headway.

Whoever the heck this Tiffany female is was damn sure getting a lot of play from not only Tariq, but Ghostman as well. Detective Dugan made a mental note as he jotted down her name. *I need to not only find out who she is and where she is, but have a long talk with her. And whoever this last number called from Tariq's cell to "B" might be the link that can shed some light on his connection to Ghostman other than this Tiffany person.*

Having had his people perform reverse number searches on "Tiffany's" and "B's" phones, unfortunately, the exhausted detective came up empty-handed. Of course, he could simply dial the two different numbers on a dry mission, fish around for answers . . . and run the risk of scaring the people off. Or he could do a little background hustle on the owners and see how they'd react when he dropped the information he'd gained on them. Kinda like a surprise attack, throwing them off guard.

Using the social media apps Tariq had on his cell, Detective Dugan was now surfing through the deceased young man's Facebook and Instagram pages. Although he hadn't updated either site in months, it still shed some light on him and the people he ran with. Going through all the photo albums, he finally hit the one marked "family and friends." While Richmond was a big city, some of the faces seemed somewhat familiar, but a few in particular stood out. *I know this damn girl and guy from someplace, but where?* The detective racked his overworked brain as pictures of Bunny and Spoe popped up on the deceased man's phone screen. For the time being, it had yet to dawn on him it was the face of the other dead body that'd washed up on the river and his girl's sister Bunny. Lying down on one of the cots in the rear of the police station, Detective Dugan decided to rest his mind and body. He'd put fresh eyes on the entire case when he woke up. Still behaving like a lovesick teenager, he texted Simone. Good morning, before he drifted off to sleep.

    Ginger, Bunny, and Simone all slept under Me-Ma's roof so they could keep a watchful eye on not only their mentally drained sister Tallhya but on Deidra and Lenny as well. Tallhya had yet to mutter one single solitary word since trying to silence their mother once and for all. Out of the four of the siblings, it was no great secret; she was the weakest. Anxiety and panic attacks were part of her extreme depression that stemmed from her being overweight and often teased as a child. Having been the first of the four of them to marry brought Tallhya a small bit of pride, but Walter's bastard love child and betrayal robbed her of that aspect of her life, along with the lump sum of her savings. Thank God she'd taken the monthly payout from the lottery and would not be completely destitute. But for now, in this unpredictable state, Tallhya was no good to her family or herself.

    The joint decision was made between her two sisters and brother that she should be committed for observation at the mental hospital. Having tried to end her own life twice before, she was no stranger to the facility. Although Bunny suggested she might make mention of the bank robbery and the fact they were holding Deidra and Lenny hostage in the basement, Simone reassured the pair the physicians would have Tallhya so doped up she would be claiming Mickey Mouse was the president of the United States and Snow White was his first lady.

    Leaving Ginger and Bunny to hold the house down, Simone placed Tallhya in her Neon and drove off. Only a block away from Me-Ma's house Simone received a text from Chase saying, Good morning, indicating he'd been up all night. Instead of smiling that the man she was dating was thinking about her, she exhaled, knowing the detective he was still hadn't discovered her secret.

"Sis, you know what's really good, don't you?"

"No, what?" Bunny glanced up from staring at pictures of her and Spoe on her cell.

"We should go down there and just kill the rotten bitch and get it over with. Both her and him," Ginger motioned toward the closed basement door. "I don't know why we wasting time keeping them alive. Y'all know we can't trust Momma or her slimeball man."

Bunny agreed, but just as she was attempting to choke Deidra out the evening before, she couldn't bring herself to actually complete the horrid act. "I swear I know you right. And I wish I could, but the dirty broad still is our mother."

"Yeah, so . . ."

"I mean, dang, maybe we could find another way."

"Another way to do what? Let her wild ass go run and tell the police on us or what? Give her all our money and just say fuck what we had to go through to get it? I don't know how you living, but with me, the struggle is real."

"Naw, Ginger, I mean maybe we could make some sort of deal with her."

"A deal?"

"Yeah, a deal. Like maybe we can offer her some of the money if she keeps her mouth shut. I mean, she already hurt, and it ain't like she could run off at the mouth anytime soon."

"Bunny, are you fucking serious right now? You can't be!"

"Yes, she might take some money and go. Leave us alone for good."

"Yeah, okay, then go broke and keep coming back for more bread, draining our black asses dry until it ain't none left. Stop bugging!"

"But, Ginger—"

"But Ginger my perfect silicone-injected ass! Girl, you know good and damn well Momma and that nothing-ass nigga she running with ain't going for that bullshit. And if you really believe that for one second, you crazier than Tallhya's nut-cake ass! They gonna need a room for two! Or did you forget her jaw was knocked the hell off and her no-good shit of a man is also a bloody mess?"

They both giggled at what Ginger said; then Bunny got somber going on to explain that in between Spoe and Tariq getting set up by some random tramp and murdered and Me-Ma collapsing on the church stage, she'd experienced enough death for the time being. If there was a way to avoid Deidra and Lenny getting killed to keep all four of them safe and sound, not to mention free from prison, then great. Bunny was all for it. However, if there was a slight chance that couldn't happen, then her mother and Lenny were both as good as dead.

After their lopsided debate on Deidra's fate, the pair decided to go down into the basement to check on the two conniving crooks. With each creak of the old wooden stairs, Bunny heard muffled sounds coming from the corner where Deidra and Lenny were tied up at. Getting closer, she noticed Lenny had somehow wiggled his hands free from the extension cord and was working on freeing his feet. Terrified of what was going to happen when Deidra's children found out he was trying to escape, Lenny didn't say a word as he stared up into Bunny's face. Hoping for some sort of compassion from the girl, he finally muttered the words he was sorry. Before Bunny could respond, Ginger cut him off, going straight ham.

"Listen up, motherfucker! I know your ass sorry now, but it's too late for all that. You wanna be so damn gangster with our momma like y'all some old played out Bonnie and Clyde, then okay then. That's on you. So deal with the consequences of the bullshit!" Balling up his fist, Ginger socked Lenny in the side of his temple, causing him to black out.

"Okay, Bunny. Help me tie this nickel-slick Negro back up. This time, I'm using this duct tape that was on the shelf. Let me see him get loose from this!" Wrapping the grey tape around his wrist five or six times, Ginger then used the remainder on Lenny's mouth, not wanting to hear his begging voice. "Beg for mercy now, you old fart!" Slowly, he grinded the heel of his shoe deeply into Lenny's backside, undoubtedly breaking the skin. "You'll know the next time to not roll out with our momma!"

"Ginger, come over here," Bunny spoke out using her cell phone as a light. "Look at her; at her face. It got bigger."

Ginger left Lenny alone for the time being and focused on Deidra. Doing as Bunny asked, he leaned over to get a good look. "Damn! You ain't never lied, but hey. God don't like ugly, so there you have it."

"Hold up, Ginger," Bunny reached for his arm as he started to head for the stairs. "We just can't leave her down here like this. It looks like her jaw is infected or some shit like that. And look at her lips. They starting to look almost bluish."

"Good, let them lying lips of hers turn all the way blue. Shiddd, let them turn black. Like I told you in the kitchen, I'm tired of giving a fuck about people who don't give a fuck about me, and that includes her! Now on that note, I'm outta here."

Bunny watched Ginger storm up the stairs. Considering her options, she decided to just try to say fuck it like him and do the same. They'd come too far to head back; besides, she had other things she had to take care of. With thoughts of Spoe heavy on her mind, Bunny double-checked her mother's restraints before saying what she believed were her final good-byes. She might've not been able to speak her final peace with Spoe or Me-Ma, but she'd have satisfaction when it came to her mother.

"You were never a mother to any of us. All we ever wanted was for you to love us. You just never took time to do it like any normal mother would. I guess we weren't good enough, huh?" Bunny lowered herself down to her mother's swollen face and continued, "Don't worry, Deidra, your lying, scheming, no-good ass going to get what's coming to you. I bet you trying to scheme up some plan right now, but guess what? It ain't gonna work. See ya, wouldn't want to be ya!" With those last words to her so-called mother, she climbed up the stairs to be with Ginger.

"Bunny, what took your ass so long? You better not be feeling sorry for that rotten piece of shit down there." Ginger rolled his eyes, hoping he didn't have to tie her ass up as well until Simone got back. He made a mental note to let Simone know how Bunny was acting.

"Ain't nothing—damn! I don't no way feel sorry for her. She deserves everything that happens to her. I'm going upstairs."

CHAPTER FIVE

Like Tallhya, Bunny was also mentally drained. Maybe not to the point she required medical attention, but enough to pop a few sleeping pills to get her through the night. Praying for inner peace and strength since the night the love of her life left to meet up with Tariq, she grew sick to her stomach. Even though she was a mourning female, she was a soldier putting on a good front. She was devastated living with the agonizing fact she'd never see Spoe alive again. Denied even the common courtesy or opportunity to view her live-in man's body before his vindictive estranged mother had him cremated, Bunny was dizzy with grief needing closure.

Always ready to get on a ra-ra tip with folk if they got out of pocket, she wanted nothing more than to get revenge on everyone involved in his murder. The fact that Ghostman had gotten killed after she planted the evidence of the bank robbery was of no comfort. Bunny still wanted to come face-to-face with the grimy bitch Tiffany she knew set her man and his best friend up. That stripper ho was the only trick Tariq had been banging recently and had gone as far as even allowing the sack-chasing chick to spend more than two nights in a row at his crib; something he never did.

Tariq used to tell Spoe everything, and in return, Spoe would fill her in. So she knew about the plan to rob some dude that Tiffany claimed was an easy come up. The only thing that bothered Bunny was Tiffany had told

Tariq the guy who they were stealing from was some dreadlock cat from New York named Dino that live right outside the county; not some Italian kingpin. Bunny had to know what happened and why. And since Spoe, Tariq, and Ghostman were all dead, the only one that could answer those questions was the forever-scheming Tiffany. Bunny knew that was the bum bitch the night she dropped the cash off to Ghostman; the one that was looking her up and down before Tariq got shot. One minute she wanted to keep it calm and let the cops do their job, while the other part wanted to run up to Treats Gentleman's Club where she knew the ill-intentioned female worked. Trying to get her mind right and deal with the loss of two of the most important people in her life, Spoe and Me-Ma, Bunny wasn't thinking clearly as her emotions were on a roller coaster.

"That's it. I'm through being a victim. That shit is for the birds." Bunny was done crying, feeling sorry for herself. Her man wouldn't want her to be weak. Spoe would want her to make each motherfucker involved in his demise to pay. She knew she couldn't rest until she found out what exactly happened to him that night. And since Spoe, Tariq, and Ghostman weren't alive to tell the awful tale, the only other person who knew what truly jumped was the dirty tramp that orchestrated the entire deadly night: Tiffany.

After making sure the clip was full in one of Spoe's guns she'd begun carrying since his death, Bunny was ready to resume being the beautiful grey-eyed beast she was born to be. "Tonight, I'm going to pay that sneaky whore a little visit down at that club she works at. I know that was her at Ghostman's house looking me up and down like she had an attitude. And if not, one of them bitches down there gonna point her sneaky ass out!" Bunny had to calm her nerves. She had a long day ahead of her and an even longer night. Placing her pistol underneath her pillow, she decided to take a short nap until Simone returned with an update on Tallhya.

The house was finally quiet. Simone was gone, still dealing with the Tallhya situation, and Bunny was upstairs taking a much-needed nap. As Ginger kicked off his shoes, he reached for the television remote. Enjoying a moment to gather his thoughts, he surfed through the channels, finally deciding to watch an episode of *The Price Is Right* in honor of Me-Ma. Just before Ginger was ready to make his guess on the final showcase, he was interrupted by three or four knocks at the front door.

"Who in the hell?" Peeking out the white sheer curtains, Ginger saw it was none other than the infamous Pastor Street. "Oh no! Not this fake-ass Negro!" Going over to check that the basement door was securely shut, Ginger finally came back into the living room asking, "Who is it?"

"Hello, there. It's Pastor Cassius Street."

"Yes?" Ginger said through the still closed door.

"I wanted to discuss something with you girls if that's okay."

"Like what?" Ginger glanced back over her shoulder to see who had won their showcase.

"Well, can I come in, please? It won't take long."

Finally cracking the door, Ginger stepped front and center. Just as beautiful as his sisters and oozing triple the amount of sex appeal, he licked his lips, informing the man of the cloth that he was the only one home. "I mean, I don't know what you wanna say that hasn't already been said, but if you wanna come in and give me a little one-on-one Bible Study, I'm down. I'm here by myself and open to your word."

Pastor Street had a lump in his throat as he took in a full-length look at Ginger. His long, perfectly shaped legs. His full, pouty lips. The inviting curve of his hips. And the enticing way Ginger stuck his finger in the side of his mouth as he spoke. Pastor Street was definitely intrigued by what he saw. He wasn't fooled one second by who Ginger truly was underneath those female clothes that hugged his body so tightly. Me-Ma had made Gene's sexual preference no huge secret. But that didn't turn the good pastor off; in truth, it turned him on. It was common, unspoken knowledge Cassius Street was a tad bit promiscuous when it came to the single women in his congregation . . . and rumored, a few of the married ones as well. But even though his flamboyant style of dress made some whisper that he was possibly a homosexual on the down low, no one had actual facts, just juicy idle gossip. However, Ginger was different from the rest. His gaydor went off immediately the first time he walked in the church and saw the good pastor prancing and dancing around the pulpit.

"Ummm . . . one-on-one?" He fought his most time-hidden demonlike desires the best he could, but felt himself growing weaker. If there was an opportunity to surface his true desire, he wasn't going to let it walk on by.

"Yes, that's right, Pastor." Ginger licked his lips while tugging down on his tight-fitting T-shirt. "You don't wanna come inside and bless me? Lay hands on me?"

Forgetting the true reason for his impromptu visit, Pastor Street threw caution to the wind. Stepping through the threshold of the door, his manhood twitched in anticipation of what Ginger had in store for him. Although this wasn't his first time at the rodeo, so to speak, this was the first time he was willing to walk on the dark side so close to home. But there was something about Ginger that was calling his name.

"Sooooooo, you're here alone, huh? Where is every-one this fine morning?" His demons were itching to see the light, and he was all for it.

"Yup, I'm here all by my lonesome. All of my sisters are gone doing what they do," he lied, knowing Bunny was upstairs sleeping.

"Oh yeah?" Cassius grinned as his palms started to sweat and his manhood twitched even more.

"Yup, just me, myself, and I," Ginger flirted, getting closer in his personal space. "And, of course, now you."

Cassius felt his manhood jump once more. As it started to slightly bulge out his trousers, Ginger, with one thing on his mind, got even closer. Pushing the envelope, he then reached his hand down, slowly stroking the pastor's rock-hard stick through his clothes. Receiving absolutely no resistance whatsoever, Ginger seductively unzipped his pants. Using one hand, he pulled his dick out and smiled with satisfaction.

"Hmmmm . . ." Cassius moaned as Ginger's hands made contact with his skin. He wanted nothing else but to feel Ginger's warm lips wrapped around his throbbing dick.

"Yesssss, baby, that's right. Hmmmm . . ." Ginger was pleasantly surprised the pastor's dick was as thick and long as it was. At that point, he could easily see why all the women in the church were going crazy over this man. Before you knew it, Ginger had dropped down to his knees and was giving Pastor Cassius Street the blow job of a lifetime, right in Me-Ma's living room. He wasn't too worried about Bunny interrupting his scene. He just hoped she would be in la-la land till they were all done.

CHAPTER SIX

Simone pulled her rust-bucket struggle-buggy Neon in front of the house just as Pastor Street was walking off the porch. Not sure of what he wanted in the first place, or worse, what he might've discovered in her grandmother's basement, she hesitatingly jumped out of her vehicle. Ready to beg him not to go to the authorities and expose their family secrets, Simone braced herself. "Pastor Street, what are you doing here?"

"Oh, hello, Simone. I really can't talk right now. I must go. I have an important meeting to attend." Stuttering and in panic because of Simone pulling up when she did, he was hella nervous and just wanted to get out of there.

"Huh, excuse me?" she said, confused by the pastor's words and actions.

"Umm, yeah. I can't talk at the present. I have some other business to handle on my agenda today." He looked at his wristwatch as a frantic expression graced his face. His steps couldn't be any faster than a person chasing after a hundred-dollar bill flying down the street.

Simone was totally taken aback. Here this man who spent his life, so it seemed, conning people and always attempting to get in her pants, was busting his ass to leave just as she pulled up. She couldn't understand why he wouldn't slow down enough to explain why he was even here so early in the day in the first place. Was he on his way to the police station? Would she and her sisters all be locked up and on the front page of tomorrow's newspaper? What would Chase say? Question after question raced through her brain as Pastor Street promised to get back in touch with her and her sisters as soon as he possibly could. After that brief verbal exchange, God's servant jumped in his expensive congregation-paid-for vehicle. With the dumbest expression ever known to man, he peeled off as if he was some wild teenager showing out on the block.

Simone sprinted up the walkway. Taking two steps at a time, she ran onto the porch. Busting through the front door as if she was the police conducting a raid, she shouted out for Ginger and Bunny. "Hey, y'all. Where y'all at? Hey!" Simone made sure the basement door was still locked.

"Damn, sis. Why you so loud? What you yelling for?" Ginger smirked, coming out of the bathroom with a bottle of mouthwash in his hands.

"What am I yelling for? Excuse the hell outta me, but did I or did I not just see that damn, no-good, nosy Pastor Street coming out of this house?"

"Pastor Street? Really?" Ginger played dumb, making Simone more agitated.

"Look, fool, stop playing dumb with me. What in the fuck did he want? He didn't go near the basement, did he? Matter of fact, tell me he didn't even come in the kitchen."

"Naw, sis. He ain't come in the kitchen," Ginger teased, waving the green-colored bottle around. "He came in my mouth!" He busted out with laughter.

Simone's facial expression needed no words. She couldn't believe what Ginger was saying or claiming that had taken place. "Okay, so are you telling me that you, Gene, gave Pastor Street some head? Is that what in the hell you standing here saying? You ain't serious, are you?"

Ginger smiled, sucking his teeth. "Yessssss, girl. Right there where you standing. Shiddd, I had his ass catching the Holy Ghost. He asked Jesus to help him as he busted. Sis, I had him promise to take a special love offering for my fine ass."

"Noooooooo," Simone laughed, holding her stomach.

"Yup, and believe it or not, Pastor got some good dick. Hell, I might even start going to church just to get another special offering!"

"Ginger, you lying." Simone couldn't stop smiling.

Bunny came down the stairs wiping her eyes. "Naw, the nasty tramp ain't lying. I thought I heard voices earlier and came down here."

"Say what?" Ginger was not the least bit embarrassed. "Well, I hope your spying ass took notes on how to give fabulous head, because, honey, I'm that real deal! You natural-born females ain't got shit on my jaw game!"

"Oh my God, Ginger, girl, please cut it out," Bunny giggled at his outlandish statements. "Naw, crazy bitch, I ain't take notes, but I did take candid camera video of y'all animal asses going at it." Holding up her cell, Bunny pushed play, showcasing Me-Ma's entrusted pastor and appointed executor of her estate with his pants down past his knees with Ginger, a known transsexual, sucking him off.

Simone fell back on the couch. "See, now, *that's* what I'm talking about. Bunny got his snake butt on video. Now let's see him try to sell this house right from underneath us. I swear if he try that mess, it's gonna be some real scandal-time shit jumping off at Sunday service next week!" Simone had Bunny send the illicit video to her and Ginger's e-mail and as text messages just for backup.

For the first time since her father died, Simone finally felt as if she'd caught a break. Taking a deep breath, then exhaling, she was relieved the pastor hadn't seen Deidra and Lenny, but she knew they had to get both of them out of that basement. After having Tallhya committed, claiming she was hearing and seeing things, Simone had a long time to think on the drive home. As much as she hated the thought of any person dying by her hand, especially her own mother, Simone knew death was the only option pending.

"Look, y'all, I don't know how y'all really feel about that situation down *there*," she nodded toward the basement door, "but we can't risk keeping them tied up much longer. We gonna mess around and get caught up. Remember what I told y'all when we was about to rob the bank . . . in and fucking out as soon as possible."

Ginger was the first to respond, repeating what he'd told Bunny earlier. "Okay, Simone, it's like this. I don't give a flying fish fuck about Momma. As far as I'm concerned, she been dead. So to me, it's nothing. I'll cut the bitch throat myself if y'all need me to step up. Hell, Lenny's too!"

Only needing Bunny to make the decision to murder their mother in cold blood unanimous, Simone and Ginger waited patiently. As Bunny focused on the screen of her cell, the once diva-minded female scrolled by, picture after picture, of her and Spoe. The more pictures she saw of them happy and smiling, the more infuriated she became. With each passing breath, her temper increased. The harsh realization she'd never see her baby, Spoe, again, was more than she could stand. The nap she'd taken earlier had only made her sorrow worse. As her heart raced, Bunny's eyes started to turn beet red. Her life would never be the same without Spoe, and no amount of money from some bank robbery she and her sisters had pulled off would make it better.

Leaping up from Me-Ma's favorite chair, she bolted into the kitchen. As a shocked Simone and Ginger tried to trail behind her, Bunny snatched up the same razor-sharp butcher knife out of the wooden block her sister had used the night before to cut up the old sheet in the basement. Flinging the basement door wide open, the doorknob slammed into the kitchen wall, causing a small piece of plaster to fall from the ceiling. Not even bothering to turn the light switch on, Bunny ran down the stairs. Simone and Ginger looked at each other, not sure if Bunny was true to her actions. No sooner than her bare feet touched the concrete floor, she headed into the corner of the basement. Kicking the box of Christmas decorations out of the way, Bunny's demeanor was unsympathetic. Callously seeing a now-conscious Lenny trying to speak from behind the duct tape, Bunny went to work as if she was a butcher slaughtering a hog.

Huddled in the other far corner of the mildew-smelling basement, Simone and Ginger were silent, never before seeing their sister in this bizarre state of mind. Trying to avoid the massive amounts of blood and mucus that was splattering everywhere, the pair of them wanted to stop Bunny and calm her down but couldn't bring themselves to get in the way of the unpredictable flying blade. Momentarily pausing, Bunny seemed to examine her handiwork on what was once Lenny before turning her attention on Deidra, who was barely clinging to life anyway. Bunny decided to take matters in her own hands and speed her mother on her way.

Clutching the brown knife handle with both hands, Bunny smirked with devilish glee as she raised the butcher knife high, almost touching the low ceiling. "I miss you, Spoe! I miss you, Spoe! I just wanna see you again! I just wanna touch you! I miss you, bae! I love you! You hear me, Spoe? I love you!" With each emotional, tormented word rolling off her quivering lips, Bunny brought the sharp object down rapidly, digging it into the Deidra's upper torso. "I just wanna be with you! I wanna hear you say I love you! Please, Spoe! Please!" Yanking it in and out of the surely dead Deidra's bleeding skin, Bunny then struck the top of her mother's head, and several times ripped open both legs, then ended her gory rampage by lodging the entire shiny blade directly into the heart of the woman who'd given her birth.

Finally out of breath and energy, Bunny became eerily silent. Taking a few steps backward, she causally dropped the butcher knife to the floor. She didn't blink. She didn't move. She didn't show any regret. Not bothering to explain her heinous actions, she then turned to disturbingly acknowledge Simone and Ginger who were still posted in the corner, speechless and in shock. As if on cue, Bunny, covered in two different blood types, crept up the stairs, leaving a trail of bloody footsteps to the bathroom. The murderess got into the shower as if she'd not just bludgeoned to death her mother, Deidra, and Lenny, the man who wanted to be down with their conniving mother.

"Oh my fucking God," Ginger shockingly pressed his hand to his chest.

"You right. Oh my God! I don't know what to say! What the fuck!"

"Girl, what in the hell was that? Better yet—*who* in the hell was that?"

"Who you asking? It was like Bunny was in some sort of strange-ass trance or something. I mean . . . She was acting more zoned out and crazy than Tallhya was last night." Simone shook her head in total disbelief.

"You mean, crazier than you running up on Lenny taking that old-ass gun from him." Ginger gave his sister the side eye and cracked a sarcastic smile, not knowing what else to do or say. "You mean crazier than that shit! Shidddd, I hope that cray cray garbage ain't floating through my DNA! 'Cause if it is, Tallhya gonna have a roommate real soon."

Simone placed her hand on Ginger's shoulder and returned the smile. "Don't worry, Gene, something tells me your DNA is safe."

Standing there a couple of minutes more trying to take in and process what had truly taken place, Simone and Ginger said a little prayer in honor of the very few good moments they'd shared with their now-deceased, selfish, unfit mother. When Deidra Banks wasn't out running the streets chasing dreams that would never come true, she was all right. But those times were limited. Now she was gone and never coming back to cause havoc in their lives ever again.

Wasting no more time going back down memory lane, they had to think quickly and move even quicker. Although they were worried about being disturbed while they were cleaning up the horror-movie-worthy scene, Simone was concerned about Bunny's erratic behavior that made her step off into the deep end like she'd just done. Confused watching her sister go from laughing and joking to heinously butchering two people in a matter of moments was incomprehensible. Zero to a hundred was an understatement in this case.

A lot of things had happened to all the Banks over the course of a month. Each sibling had done a lot of questionable, over-the-top stuff to survive the best way they saw fit. However, this act Bunny had just committed was far most the wildest. Now she was upstairs in the shower humming a love song while she washed their mother's blood splatters off her face. She had just turned causally crazy, just like Tallhya. Simone and Ginger joked they hoped that wasn't a family trait, but getting a closer look at their sister's handiwork, Simone secretly prayed it really wasn't—and if it was, that the bullshit missed her. Before they could get it together and deal with how to get Deidra and Lenny out of the house, they could hear Bunny's footsteps tapping toward the front door. They both looked at each other, waiting on who would stop her from heading out the door. But before either one made the attempt to do so, they heard the front door slam and a car pulling off, heading to God knows where.

Gathering all the old blankets and sheets they could find in Me-Ma's house, Ginger grabbed two pair of gloves and, ironically, considering the unholy job they were doing, an old "God Is Good" T-shirt to serve as a mask. Simone checked both the deceaseds' pockets for any ID's or personal items. Using a small hand ax, she chopped off their hands with intentions of dumping them separately from the bodies, making it harder to identify them with no fingerprints. After drinking almost a quarter of a bottle of Rémy to get his rattling nerves together, Ginger, along with Simone, started the awful task of not only wrapping the bodies up, but also scrubbing any traces of the murders from the floors and walls. Using all the bleach and other cleaning aids they could find, they disinfected the entire area.

Immediately noticing Deidra's and Lenny's blood seeping through the many sheets and blankets each was surrounded with, Ginger knew transporting the corpses couldn't take place until someone made a trip to their local Home Depot. Otherwise, the trunks of their vehicles would be soiled with evidence to two murders. Switching gears, Ginger instantly went into survival mode by any means necessary—which translated into *"Bitch, stay your black pretty ass out of prison."* As much as Gene loved men and what they had dangling between their legs as he morphed into Ginger, prison was not an option. He ran upstairs after informing Simone he'd be right back.

Thirty minutes later, he returned with three gigantic rolls of double ply industrial painters' plastic. Much to his and Simone's delight, after making sure both bodies were Saran-wrapped totally, the leakage of Deidra's and Lenny's body fluids was contained.

Solemnly, the blank-faced siblings began the grueling task of trying to get their mother and her boyfriend up the basement stairs. After what seemed like a lifetime of pulling, pushing, yanking, and kicking—thank God or the devil—their prayers were answered. Phase one of their disposal plan was complete. Ginger and Simone threw them onto the rear enclosed porch like two bags of garbage waiting for pickup. Unrolling an oil-stained carpet remnant from the corner of the porch, Simone further concealed their unfortunate victims from any prying eyes. Waiting for the right opportunity, they would toss them into the back of an older model van Ginger borrowed from some nine-to-five workingman he often tricked with. Dumping their problems off in a random place was the plan. Then, hopefully, they could find out what was up with Bunny going off like a caged serial murderer possessed with everything bad.

CHAPTER SEVEN

Detective Chase Dugan was still extremely exhausted. He was drained, not only physically, but mentally as well. He'd pulled an all-nighter working on what he felt was the ultimate case of a lifetime. The brief nap he'd intended on taking in the rear of the squad room almost easily turned into a full-pledged eight hours of sleep. Trying desperately to find a link between the two back-to-back bank robberies was a tedious task, to say the least. With a town full of closed-lipped folk adhering to the "no-snitch" policy, he had to depend on good old plain police work.

There were no major shortcuts this time around. Locking his fingers behind his head, he leaned back ready to do mind battle. Posted at his desk, hoping for a break-through, he once again started to examine the seized cell phone. Tapping the blue-colored icon, he was back on Tariq's Facebook page. Not a rookie to the social media game, the detective picked up where he'd left off at. Hell-bent on a mission, he continued navigating through hundreds of pictures in numerous albums. Besides the faces that seemed somewhat familiar to him from earlier, the young victim had an extensive number of pictures and selfies with the same background. Tapping the decent-size cell screen, the pictures became bigger. The bigger they became, the resolution diminished. However, thanks to the detective's 20/20 eyesight, along with being able to zoom in even more on various parts of the pictures, he smiled. He'd finally found a common denominator from Tariq and Ghostman's cellular devices that might link them together in other ways. Apparently, each one of the now-deceased men had strong attractions to strippers that worked at Treat's Gentlemen's Club. One in particular: Tiffany, who just had a huge birthday celebration a few weeks prior.

Hell, yeah! This what I'm talking about! Finally, some sort of break for the kid. I was starting to question my damn self. I knew if I just took my ass to sleep for a little while I'd be good to go. Shiddd . . . It's a good thing I did because it seems like I'ma be taking a trip down to the club later. With a crooked smirk of satisfaction on his face, he tossed the cell on the desk and went to pour himself a cup of strong coffee.

With other officers starting their shift, Detective Dugan filled a few of them in on what he planned on doing later that evening. "Man, I'm telling you, despite all the long crazy hours and bullshit we gotta put up with from the citizens, I love this job. I mean, damn, what other type of gig can have you going to chill at the strip club and get paid to do so? I mean, what can your wife or girl say? You on the clock; city time . . . making money."

One of the married men on the team laughed at his colleague. "You real funny, dude; a real comedian. But why don't you get you a wife—hell, or even a woman, for that matter? Then come talk that bullshit about going to see some seminude female other than your girl and think it's gonna be all good at home. We'll all be bringing you flowers to the hospital!"

Laughing himself at what was said, Detective Dugan realized that hours upon hours had flown by, and he had yet to hear Simone's beautiful voice. He liked her like he'd liked no other woman in an extremely long amount of time. There was something about her from day one that had penetrated the body armor he had built around his heart. Now, just like that, in a matter of days, the educated, poised, bank teller had broken through. Not wanting to lose Simone Banks like he'd done other females in the past from neglect of time due to his dedication to his job, he reached in his pocket, removing his own cell. Going to sit out in his car for a little privacy, he turned on his favorite radio station. With the soulful music playing softly, Chase dialed Simone's number.

It was finally quiet at Me-Ma's house. After all the things that'd taken place since her abrupt death, her grandkids knew she had to be turning over in that fresh grave she was lying in. Yet, some of the factors were put directly into motion by Me-Ma's own hand reaching out from the ground. Leaving not only her money, but the family house as well to Pastor Cassius Street had set off a shitload of events that might not have taken place if her grandkids had other options in place. Playing the unfair hand that was dealt to them, at this point, it was what it was.

Ginger and Simone had both taken showers. The exhausted pair was eager to get their mother's and Lenny's blood mixed with their own sweat washed off of them. It'd been the longest twenty-four-hour time span they'd ever lived through . . . robbing a bank, setting up Ghostman to get knocked, then ultimately murdered, having to subdue their greedy mother and her dim-witted man, watching Bunny slaughter their asses, then damn near breaking their backs dragging their heavy, chopped-up bodies out to the back porch. Simone also had to get Tallhya committed. And lastly, Ginger was extra tired having secured that Pastor Street wouldn't be trying any gank moves on the house the Banks siblings called home.

"No shade, but I still can't believe Bunny bugged out like that!"

"Who in the fuck is you telling?" Ginger replied, rubbing baby lotion on both his swollen feet. "And then got the nerve to play that fraud-ass crazy role."

"Yeah, and then disappear, leaving us to clean her mess up." Simone sat back on the couch chopping it up with Ginger as if they hadn't just witnessed their mother take her last breath. "I keep calling her, and it's going straight to voice mail."

Ginger shook his head while shrugging his shoulders. "Oh well, unless you wanna take another trip out to the crazy house today where Tallhya's at, let that bitch Bunny be. She'll get over it sooner or later. That bullshit business with Spoe, Tariq, and that Ghostman motherfucker got her spooked. It got her in a place in her mind that ain't right."

"Yeah, well . . ." Before Simone could finish her sentence her cell phone rang. Instantly a gigantic smile graced her face.

"Oh my freaking God," Ginger acted as if he was throwing up in his mouth. "Let me fucking guess . . . Detective Good Dick is calling!"

Simone threw up her middle finger at Ginger.

"Hey now, Chase." Simone tried to block all her recent troubles out as she happily answered.

"Hey yourself, Miss Lady. How are you doing this evening? You good?"

"Yes, I'm good. I'm just sitting back handling a few things here at my grandmother's house," she answered, not thinking he could've asked to stop by.

Ginger sat straight up. Ear hustling, he shot Simone the serious side eye, then pointed toward the back porch where the bodies were waiting to be loaded into the borrowed van. Mouthing the words "What the fuck!"

Ginger reminded the love struck Simone to not get that
carried away with the conversation with this fool that
she forgets he's the police. Every single person in the
hood they lived in knew, at the end of the day, it was fuck
the police. They might've claimed to offer protection, but
that was only to some. And Ginger knew that if Chase had
the slightest bit of knowledge that Simone was involved
in extortion, bank robbery, and the premeditated murder
of her own mother, their fledgling love affair flight would
be over before it really got off the ground.

"Wow, girl. First things first, I wanna tell you I really
dig you. And I really enjoy spending time with you."

"Excuse me, Chase," Simone interrupted, eager for
him to get to the point. "But I know you're not breaking
up with me, are you? I mean, trying to give me the brush-
off?"

"Oh hell, naw, girl. You're not gonna get rid of me that
easy. I was just gonna say I'ma be tied up just a few more
days trying to close these robbery cases out, and I didn't
want you to think that I was ignoring you."

Simone was torn. Part of her was elated her new beau
was offering a reasonable explanation of why he would
not be as accessible as he would like to be, while the
other part of her was worried that the explanation he
gave could bite her in the ass, costing her and her siblings
their freedom. Not willing to just sit back and wait for
the unknown to occur, Simone started to question him
on the sly. "Okay, then, Chase, I was about to say . . . I
mean, to be honest, I'm really feeling you too."

"Oh yeah?" He leaned his car seat farther back after
turning the radio all the way down. "Simone, I swear I
hope you understand. I don't want you to feel some sort
of way. It's the job keeping me busy."

"Yeah, of course, I do understand that business comes
first. That goes without saying. It's just that I'm so con-

fused about the whole thing in general. I mean, I thought that god-awful man that'd robbed the bank was dead. So it's over with now . . . right? I mean, what else is there to it?"

"Well, kinda sorta. But it's not just that one case I'm working on any more. We think it might be a link to the other one." He offered her an insight on privileged police information. "So until we follow every possible lead, I'm might have to pull a few doubles. Like tonight." He dared not say he was going to a strip club, so he just kept it simple. "It might be a long crazy night for me, but I'll definitely text you later, if that's all right with you."

"Of course, it is, Chase. Keep me posted." Simone's nerves were rattled, to say the least. Hearing what should've been a closed case was now being linked with the first bank robbery had her shook. A damn crime that had absolutely nothing to do with the one they'd committed.

After ending the conversation, he returned to the station and headed to the squad room. Questioning each one of his team members to see who wanted to tag along to Treat's Gentlemen's Club, Detective Dugan had a burning need to tip one stripper in particular: Tiffany. And if luck was on his side, the do-anything-strange-for-some-change dancer would be open to answer a few questions about both the deceased men that seemed so attached to her.

Meanwhile, Simone's mouth grew dry, and she felt dizzy. Sadly, she filled Ginger in on the fact that even though Ghostman was dead and being deemed the mastermind behind the bank robbery they'd pulled off, they definitely weren't out of the woods yet. She informed a now-also-concerned Ginger that Detective Dugan and his men were not gonna leave any stone unturned until they brought every single person that played a hand in both robberies to justice. Nervously, Simone once again called Bunny to give her the update on not just what Chase had told her but the Deidra situation as well. Just like earlier, she still only got her voice mail. She tried again just for good measure but got the same outcome.

It had gotten dark enough for Simone and Ginger to complete their final task for the evening. Dressed in all-dark clothing, they each put on sneakers, lacing them tight. After Ginger walked around the house making sure the coast was clear, he signaled for his sister to open up the rear door of the porch. On the count of three, Ginger and Simone lifted Lenny's body first. Rigor mortis had set in, and he was as heavy as a sack of bricks and stiff as a board. Even though Ginger was born a man, the struggle was real. It was as if Lenny, even though semichopped up, was repaying them for his murder by being extra difficult to get down the stairs and into the back of the cargo van. Deidra, on the other hand, seemed to be a bit more cooperative. Her frame was much smaller in size, and maybe it was because Simone and Ginger were getting rid of a lifelong headache that made tossing their mother into the van a breeze.

With Ginger behind the wheel, Simone acted as the navigation system, instructing him which way to turn. Finally getting to the murky banks of the James River, Ginger backed the van up. Jumping out of the vehicle, the pair moved as quickly as possible dumping the bodies. Dousing the Home Depot plastic shroud Deidra and Lenny were wearing with lighter fluid, Ginger grabbed a few twigs and lit the ends. Using the twigs as small torches, he dropped them on top of the two. Not waiting to see the certain bonfire-like blaze burn, they rushed back to the van and hit the road. About one mile from the river, Simone set the Ziploc freezer bag containing four hands on fire. Knowing the police would think it was just some random bad-ass kids setting a Dumpster on fire, she tossed the bag in a school garbage can that was full of paper, making the hands burn even faster. In less than ninety minutes after they'd left the house, Simone and Ginger were back at home; no worries; no remorse; no regrets.

Focused on what would be their next move, they both headed upstairs for a much-needed nap to recharge.

CHAPTER EIGHT

I'm done! I swear I'm so fucking done with the dumb bullshit! Ain't no bitch or punk-ass nigga gonna take advantage of me any damn more. I let Spoe into my heart, and he left me. He let these fucking streets take him away from me; away from this house; this bed. I don't even know how he took his last breath. What was he saying? What was he thinking? Did he suffer? I know that idiot Ghostman shot Tariq, but where was my baby? Where was Spoe? Oh my God! Shit! Now I'm fucked all the way up! And why? 'Cause some greedy sack-chasing trick-ass pole swinger was trickin' on my man! This some real bullshit!

Bunny used her feet to kick off the thin but expensive comforter that'd been surrounding her since she stepped foot back inside her condo. The condo that once belonged to her and her man . . . her best friend and confidant. Spoe was supposed to be her hustle partner for life, and now she was forced to be out here flying solo. *That ho Tiffany gonna pay for settin' my man and Tariq up. She thinks it's over? Like Ghostman gonna be dead, and it's all good?* Bunny's mind had been spinning all afternoon. From the point she snapped and sent her mother and Lenny on their way, she'd been harping on the night Spoe left her arms until the moment Ghostman callously announced he was dead. Since that moment, Bunny felt as if she never had a second to slow down and take in what'd truly taken place. Then just like that, when she heard Ginger and Simone talking, she snapped. It was too much yakking and not enough action. She'd killed two people without the smallest bit of remorse. And now, it was the stripper's time to pay. When Bunny got down to Treat's Gentlemen's Club, she was gonna be hell-bent on damn near wrapping that pole Tiffany swung from around her neck—twice.

"Hit the strip club, we be letting bands go. Everybody hating, we just call them fans though. In love with the money, I ain't never letting go . . ."

"All right, y'all get your hands out your pants and make it rain on some of these hot-box pretty young things running around this motherfucker tonight. Money in the air makes them legs open wide! Let's see some legs and cash in the air!" The DJ was earning every bit of his salary trying to coax some of the tighter fist pussy-gawkers to cough up some of the dough they were sitting on.

"Girl, I don't know what in the hell is wrong with some of these crab-ass niggas tonight. They acting like the world coming to an end, and they need to hold onto every dollar they can get their hands on," Tiffany remarked, hesitant to even get undressed and hit the stage. "Shiddd, I might as well go back to the crib and chill for the rest of the evening. Watch some damn cable or something. You know what I mean? This may not be worth it."

Sable sat across from the tall top table agreeing with everything her homegirl was saying. Nursing the same glass of cheap wine she'd paid for herself since stepping foot in the club, she wanted to do the same as Tiffany. "I swear, I'm telling you, I was about five minutes away from bouncing outta this dried-up spot my damn self. But you know Cash Dreams having her party tonight."

"Oh yeah. I freaking forgot. Especially considering it's so whack in here." Tiffany turned up her lip, then rolled her eyes.

"Yeah, I know, right?" Sable giggled out loud snapping her fingers to the music blasting out of the built-in speakers. "But the dumb bitch did support my party and yours, so you know how that bullshit goes. Even if she can't pack the house, we gonna show the skank some love. You already know."

"Yeah, I do. Shit!"

"Well, sis, stop fucking complaining. At least your ass had a few days off relaxing and ain't been posted in this bitch! It's been crazy mad slow, for real, for real."

Tiffany walked away from the dressing area and headed to the bar and ordered a double shot of top-shelf Hennessey from the waitress. Quickly downing the throat-smooth liquor, she tried to get her mind right and get back into the hustle and flow of the club life. Sable was correct. She did indeed have a few days off, but she definitely wasn't relaxing; far from it. Even though Tiffany tried to play the tough role, she was still a female and still had emotions. In between the haunting image of watching Tariq get murked and Ghostman getting his dumb self killed by the damn police, the gorgeous, conniving go-getter was ass out with two of her main sponsors now gone. Trying to be nickel slick and come up, now with both her moneymaking dudes fallen on their backs, Tiffany needed to mess around now and find some new tits to suck off of. Those revenue wells had permanently run dry, and it was only God that she believed help her dodge the bullets of getting caught up behind each one's sudden demise.

True, Tiffany had money saved, but the lavish lifestyle she wanted to live had to be maintained. She had tried repeatedly to get with her other homeboy Dino, who was

head of the infamous Bloody Lions Posse. But unfortunately for her, the seasoned criminal moneymaker Dino
wasn't returning her calls. She prayed he didn't have
a clue she'd low-key sent Spoe and Tariq to break into
his mansion and relieve him of all his drugs and cash.
Tiffany knew his crew were the ones who really killed
Spoe and not Ghostman, but either way it went, she felt
it was none of her business. Both the stickup niggas were
gonna be dead at the end of that night anyway, so it really
didn't matter by whose hand. Their fate just came a little
earlier than expected. Now she was back at the strip club
seeking her next sponsor. A true hustler is only as good as
their next mark; and Tiffany was back on the hunt.

Watching the news, Dino lit a blunt and frowned. It
had been well over a week since he'd doubled back home
and caught two crooks violating his domain. After having
an in-house shoot-out with the guys, Dino's dedicated
crew forced both of them to jump from one of the bedroom windows. Suffering bone injuries from the rough
landing, the brazen thieves fled into the woods. Swiftly
realizing they had not only a huge portion of his money,
but some of his drugs as well, Dino let his trained dogs go
in pursuit. Luckily for Dino, the two men weren't as quick
as they hoped to be. In between the darkness of the night,
the many trees, fallen limbs, and holes in the uneven
ground, the thieving duo never had a chance. It was like
taking candy from a baby. The attack dogs were on their
trail immediately and never let up until they earned the
fresh porterhouse steaks they were blessed with later that
evening. After shooting one of them from afar, Dino ran
up, finally getting satisfaction. Firing a fatal shot directly
between the eyes, he'd sent one of them home to meet his
Maker. Much to his dismay, the other unknown man got

away, taking the bag of their ill-gotten gain. Dino's loyal team searched high and low for Spoe's accomplice but sadly, came up empty-handed.

After running the deceased stickup man's pockets, they saw he had not one piece of identification on him, making the task of linking him up with another person or enemy drug-dealing crew practically impossible. There was only one way to positively identify the guy, and that was to let the trained professionals earn their paychecks: the police. Having his men toss Spoe's head-shot-wounded body into the James River, Dino swore he'd find not only the person who had his property, but the disloyal motherfucker who'd set him up in the first place. As he focused on news report after news report, he soon saw that his archrival, Marky aka Ghostman had been caught up in a bank robbery and killed by the police. *If I only had that package that was stolen, broken down and circulating in the streets, I'd been on triple-boss status right about now! Now I gotsta make a trip and make this bullshit right. I swear to God if that bum duck that rob me wasn't already floating facedown in the river, I'd shoot him in his head ten more times!*

Interrupted by the sound of his cell phone ringing, Dino looked down at the screen, annoyed when he saw yet another call from Tiffany's good gold-digging ass. *Ain't this about nothing. No wonder this hungry ho keeps calling me back-to-back like she crazy or like I owe her something. That bitch think she's superslick. I see her other meal ticket Ghostman's fag ass is deader than a motherfucker, and now she wanna come back over here and suck on daddy's chocolate pole. Like I'm some sort of fool. These bitches these days be doing the fucking most; like niggas stupid.*

Not thinking she'd have enough nerve to set him up to get robbed, Dino knew anything was possible but chose to not see the writing on the wall. Tiffany, although a do-anything-for-a-dollar type of female, was not on Dino's short list radar of who was guilty. She'd seen him and his Bloody Lions Posse deal with slum-ass dudes that crossed them on more than one occasion and couldn't fathom the thought she'd risk her life going against him, no matter who she was giving her pussy to. Dino swore on everything he loved he had Tiffany pegged. He knew she wanted some good stiff dick every so often when she wasn't into females, a few dollars to put in those overpriced handbags she liked to brag about, and get her car note paid on a monthly basis; nothing more, nothing less. He never thought she would be able to pull off something like that. Besides, she was just another gold-digging hood rat.

CHAPTER NINE

Detective Dugan and Officer Jakes pulled up in front of the semicrowded strip club. Opting not to get valet, they found a parking space on the other side of the block. Even though it was against department policy, Detective Dugan encouraged Jakes to do as he was and leave their pistols and badges hidden in the vehicle. Not wanting to be immediately marked as the police, he felt it'd be better to try to gain more information on the sly. If the bouncers knew they were 5-0, then the DJ would know. If the DJ knew, then the waitress would soon find out; then down the line until every single dancer and even the house mother would know they were cops. Of course, no one wanted to be seen gossiping with the police. Giving a lap dance and getting tipped for it was acceptable. A bitch was being about her paper. But sitting around shooting the breeze about this, that, and the other thing was out of the question. That was . . . unless you wanted to be labeled a snitch. There was already enough dead bodies washing up in the river, so to keep things tight, they were going as regular Joes.

Showing his partner for the night a printed picture of Tiffany, they both exited the car. Making sure the doors were locked, the pair made their way to the club's entrance. After allowing the bouncers to search them and paying the inflated fee to get in, Detective Dugan and Officer Jakes found an empty table. In a matter of minutes, they were seemingly swarmed by countless dancers begging them for a dance or a drink. All sorts of shapes and sizes, the two policemen discussed amongst themselves that no female that'd approached them up until this point was a real showstopper.

"Man, I ain't lying. There's a lot of these chicks that need to give up this bullshit as a career. I mean, they looking tore up from the floor up."

"You ain't lying!" Dugan easily agreed with Jakes. Sipping on his glass of fruit juice, he remarked that the weave most dancers were wearing probably cost more than the car he was driving. After sharing a few more laughs, the reason for their visit was finally called to the center stage. As the house lights lowered, the more the smoke machine kicked in. Before Chase knew it, his mouth dropped slightly open. Licking his drying lips, he stared into the face of one of the most beautiful women he'd seen in a long time. Of course, Simone Banks was a stunna in real life and his girl, so to speak. But this Tiffany girl oozed of the freaky, nasty, sexual "come-fuck-me-rough-and-hard-daddy" demeanor that only wet dreams and fantasies were made of.

Taking out Tariq's cell phone, he dialed Tiffany's number to see if she was the right girl. And as luck would have it, she took her cell out of her bag and looked at it before signaling for the DJ to start her music. Focused on every twist, turn, and spin she made on the brass pole, the man sworn to uphold the law was almost lost as to why he and Officer Jakes were there in the first place. Mesmerized by the multiple flashing lights causing the dancer's bracelet and earrings to sway, sparkle, and stand out on their own, he had to work hard to concentrate.

"They know that's mine. Bust it, baby. Everybody know that's mine. Bust it, baby. Everybody know that's mine." The music played loudly.

Shaking off the erotic trance that had him engulfed, Detective Dugan informed his boy the vivacious female that'd just shown both her breasts and was parting her perfectly plump ass cheeks to the music playing was their girl. She was Tiffany, the possible link to not only two bank robberies, but two homicides as well.

"When she comes offstage I'm going to get her to come and sit with us. Maybe buy her a drink or two and see if we can pick her brain for any info," he anxiously tapped the side of his glass with his fingertips. "Who knows, dude? Maybe with all that beauty she might be brainless. The girl might slip up and make our job that much easier."

"Yeah, you right, Chase," Jakes tried to be informal in case someone was ear hustling and could make out that they were cops.

"If we play this thing right tonight, we might both mess around and get promotions by daybreak. If not," the detective teased still eyeballing the stage and Tiffany's wide ass, "the unemployment office will be calling our names!"

Bunny had taken a long hot bath. After brushing her hair up into a messy bun, she applied her makeup as perfectly as she always did. Coming out of the huge walk-in closet, she was dressed in an outfit that Spoe loved to see her wearing. He always teased that it made her ass sit high and her tits look like they were saluting. Not knowing how the night would turn out, she packed a small overnight bag . . . just in case. Checking the floor-length mirror one last time, she left three sealed envelopes on her dresser, along with her favorite ring given to her by her beloved. Taking the framed photo of her and Spoe out of the bedroom and placing it on the mantle, she smiled. With nothing but her driver's license tucked in her lace bra, five crispy hundred-dollar bills in hand, and her designer overnight bag, Bunny Banks locked up the condo. Leaving the house keys underneath the second flower pot on the left side of the porch, she felt confident. Slowly strolling to her car, she tossed the bag into the trunk.

The revenge-minded female started the engine, then checked her cell phone for the time. *Oh, a bitch gonna pay tonight for fucking over me and my man! It's about to be some real consequences for Miss Ratchet-Ass Tiffany!* Concentrating on one thing and one thing only, she backed out of the driveway, then made her way outside of the gated community. On the way to the strip club Bunny rode in utter silence. There was no need to snap her fingers or bob her head to any music. There was no need to hear upbeat commercials about this party or that or whose upcoming concert was in the weeks to follow. She was deep off into her own zone and wanted to stay that way; at least until the vengeful task she wanted to complete was done. She had to be focused on her task at hand.

With less than five minutes away from pulling up at her destination, a strange sense of pride took over. Bunny began to have more flashbacks of the once-perfect life she and Spoe lived. The life that was now nothing more than a memory. Adding fuel to her already revengeful burning fire, Bunny relived in her mind the last time her lips touched Spoe's and the last time he told her that he'd be forever hers. Seconds later, she was in front of the club handing her car keys to the valet. When the valet asked her how long she would be, she had absolutely no response. Blessing him with one of her five hundred-dollar bills, he automatically kept it up front with her keys close by. As the ecstatic valet and every other man waiting to gain entry into the club watched her walk by, they hoped and prayed Bunny, with all her curves, was going inside to audition for one of the club headliners. After allowing herself to be searched by a dyke female bouncer, Bunny stepped into the dimly lit establishment. Adjusting her eyes, she heard the music bouncing off the walls.

"Best believe she got that good thang. She my little hood thang. Ask around, they know us. They know that's mine. Bust it, baby. Everybody know that's mine. Bust it, baby. Everybody know that's mine."

Like most men who entered the club, Bunny's attention shot to center stage. Taking a few steps toward the seminude performer, Bunny was now sure that was Tiffany. That was the dirty female that she'd seen coming out of Tariq's apartment weeks ago and the one and the same ruthless bitch that was acting all gangster when she delivered the money to Ghostman. Bunny took a deep breath. She felt every beat of the loud-playing music penetrate her entire being. She was starting to feel the exact rage she felt when Deidra left this earth; a cold emptiness. Her head was pounding. A huge lump seemed to be lodged in her throat. No matter how much she tried to swallow, it wouldn't go away. Here, this murderous setting-niggas-up home-wrecking whore was a few feet away, swinging from a pole trying to gank fools out of their money like it was business as usual. Fuck all that! Bunny's world was turned upside down. She had to make shit right for Spoe. Point-blank and period, she had to let Tiffany know what she and her man Ghostman had done to her once-perfect life. She was suffering, so now Tiffany would feel the same type of pain.

Glancing over at one of the empty tables, Bunny noticed that someone's steak dinner had arrived. Guessing the person was either one of the thirsty men at the flashing light-lit stage tipping that cash slut Tiffany or in the bathroom washing his hands, Bunny unwrapped his white cloth napkin and politely borrowed his knife. Standing back in the shadows, trying to be as inconspicuous as possible, Spoe's woman waited for Tiffany to finish her set. *That ho ain't doing no VIP dances tonight unless it's down at the county morgue!*

Detective Dugan and Officer Jakes were too busy enjoying the show Tiffany was displaying that they never noticed Bunny lurking in the shadows at the side of the stage.

"Damn, I didn't even think that was possible to do on a pole!" Detective Dungan took another sip of his fruit juice.

"You ain't lying!" Officer Jakes put his hand up for a high five.

Detective Dungan soon felt a little uneasy when two strippers came by to offer him and his friend a lap dance.

"Can we offer y'all a dance in VIP?" The strippers gave them a little tease with a shake of their asses.

Detective Dungan quickly put his hand up to stop them. "No, thanks, ladies. We already have that covered."

"Let me guess, Tiffany, right?" One of the strippers turned around before shooting them the stink eye.

"That bitch is taking the only money left in this slow-ass shallow-pocket-having club. I'm going the fuck home!" The other stripper followed suit and flipped the detectives off.

"Damn, it's brutal out here, huh?" Officer Jakes chuckled.

"We'll be out of here shortly. It's time to get this show on the road. I'll be right back." Detective Dungan walked toward the stage with a twenty-dollar bill out.

"Damn, Dungan, why do you get to have all the fun?" Officer Jakes laughed.

"It's an unfair world, my friend!" Detective Dungan shouted back.

CHAPTER TEN

Pastor Cassius Street had just finished his evening service with the church's prayer warriors. He was a little bit out of sorts, and they could easily see something was wrong but opted not to speak on it. He knew the Word of the Bible back-to-back, almost word-for-word. That was one of the many attributes he prided himself on. But this evening, he was off. Most of the scriptures he was quoting were off. Whether it was one word or the entire passage, he was off, and he was tongue-tied.

As he stood at the pulpit attempting to preach his motivational sermon, his manhood started to twitch. As much as the flamboyant preacher tried to fight off the evil, illicit thoughts of what had taken place earlier in the midmorning, he couldn't. He couldn't resist the chill bump-raising flashbacks of Ginger touching him. He closed his eyes to block out the sexually charged memory of the man who dressed as a woman caressing his body. Pastor Street didn't want to enjoy Me-Ma's grandson blessing him with the best head he'd ever experienced in life, but so be it. He had definitely enjoyed it. So much so that it was the only thought that occupied his mind and inner being since the moment he'd busted a nut and the second Ginger swallowed his seed. Now he wanted nothing more than to have all the women from the congregation that were known to do his bidding to leave. He wanted them to all say their finally good-byes so he could go into his office and stroke his meat raw while whispering Ginger's name. Having already done so twice in the bathroom, once in his car, and secretly while his parishioners were bowing their head in prayer, he knew he had to have another taste of the girlie man.

"Okay, you ladies make sure to have a blessed night. And please drive home safely. You know the devil stay working overtime out in these dangerous streets."

"Thank you, Pastor. You do the same," they all replied in unison, heading toward their vehicles in the parking lot.

Locking the church doors, without breaking stride, he retreated to the privacy of his office. Dimming the lights, Cassius relaxed, sitting back on his plush black leather couch. Getting comfortable, he repeated Ginger's name as he'd made him do while he was sucking him off. *Ginger, Ginger, oh my God, Ginger! Yes, yes, oh my God, yes, just like that!*

Unzipping his pants, the pastor groped his semihard dick. After squeezing it a few times, then yanking downward, he pulled it all the way out. Exhaling, he marveled how swollen the head was. He'd had plenty of pussy from many a woman and, shamefully, some ass from a few men, but absolutely nothing could compare to the feeling of sheer ecstasy that Ginger had brought about. Now here he was, Cassius Street, a head pastor of a major church in the city, caught up in his emotions feeling some sort of a way about another man. Hitting yet another lick, he shot his thick sperm across the room, landing it on the pages of an open Bible. *Oh my God in heaven! Save me from myself! Please, help me fight this!* The well-respected peddler of the Holy Word hoped his new obsession would not be his downfall.

Trying his very best to keep his mind on the sermon he was writing for the upcoming Sunday, Cassius's thoughts went back to Ginger. Finally giving up on fighting his urges and making love to the palm of his hand, Pastor Street licked his lips. Removing the crumbled piece of paper out of the waste paper basket his new sexual obsession had scribbled his number down on, he briefly stared at it before dialing the digits. Three rings later, the man that'd easily swallowed two loads of his juice back-to-back answered.

"Yeah, this Ginger, so speak on it."

"Hello."

"Yes."

"Hey."

"Hey, who is this?" Ginger asked with a sassy attitude as if the world belonged to him and no one should even consider disputing that fact.

"This is umm . . . umm . . ."

"Look here, who the hell ever this is?" he snapped ready to attack a possible prank caller for wasting his breath. "I ain't got time for the games. Now, final chance; who the hell is this?" After a brief silence from both him and the mystery caller, Ginger went all in for the kill. "Fuck it, I'm about to hang up on your silly self! I ain't about to play no games!"

"Wait, it's umm . . . me."

"And who the fuck is *me?*"

"Pastor Street," he hesitantly replied in a soft tone, as if someone was listening.

Ginger then recognized his voice and somewhat smiled. "Ohhh . . . hey, there, Pastor. You should've said it was you from the jump. I was about to hang up, then add this number to my blocked list of folk that work my nerves."

"Oh, well, umm . . . I'm sorry. It's just that . . ."

Ginger was used to down low dudes who pretended not to like other men being tongue-tied when they spoke to an openly gay man. They had a taste for a little roughhouse backdoor loving but didn't want to admit it to themselves—let alone the world. "Don't worry about it, Pastor. I understand. So tell me what you doing tonight?"

"Tonight?" he answered Ginger's question with a question.

"Yeah, tonight, silly. What you got going on tonight, and can I have the same thing popping as you? I'm bored as hell and ready to have some fun. You up for it?"

Thrown off by Ginger being so forward, Cassius Street's usually boisterous voice was full of confusion as he looked up at a hand carved cross hanging on the far wall of the office. "Well, I guess so. I'm just down here at the church finishing some paperwork." He couldn't help himself to the offering that was urging him all day.

"The church?" Ginger got up, reaching for his shoes, ready to roll out.

"Yes, umm . . . the church."

Ginger had a long day and night. He needed some relaxation after dragging two bodies out of the crib and dumping them. He needed something to get his mind right, and sucking the pastor off again was just what the doctor ordered. "Okay, then, sweetie. I'll be there shortly. Just hold tight and I'll hit you when I'm at the front door."

Saying a few prayers for salvation, asking God to pre-forgive him for the sins he knew he was about to commit, the good reverend felt like a kid in a candy store. Rubbing his hands together, he didn't know what to do next. Ginger would be here soon, and if he had his way, Me-Ma's grandson's lips would be blessing his manhood with his almighty power.

Throwing the various religious books he had sitting on the arm of the couch into a corner, then tossing a few extra choir robes in the closet, Cassius was ready for whatever. Going into his private bathroom, he brushed his teeth, washed off his dick, and put on a small bit of cologne. Spraying some air freshener around the medium-size room, he anxiously sat back waiting for his cell phone to ring. Twenty minutes later, the pastor's prayers were answered.

"Hey, now, bae. I'm glad you called me." Ginger wasted no time pushing his way through the front double doors into the church's inner sanctuary.

At a loss for words, Cassius nervously smiled in anticipation of the inevitable only seconds from taking place.

"Wow, it's creepy as hell in here at night, by ourself, with all the lights dimmed." Ginger sinfully pranced down the aisleway as Cassius's eyes zoomed in on his perfectly shaped ass.

"It's not that bad," he finally spoke, hoping he hadn't invited the devil inside.

Ginger had not one bit of respect for the church Me-Ma called her second home. Breezing past the area his grandmother dropped dead at, he swooped up one of the blessed prayer candles from the altar. After telling Cassius to lead the way to his office, Ginger grinned, ready to pounce on the man of the cloth.

"Here we go." He motioned for him to step into the office.

"Oh, so this is your private hangout, huh?"

"I guess you can say that."

"Well, I guess this is where you do all your private one-on-one, get-right-with-the-Lawd sessions, huh?" Ginger laughed, kicking off his shoes before plopping down on the black leather couch.

Letting his guard down, the pastor returned the laughter and stopped fighting the feeling. "Yeah, one-on-one." He wanted to jump Ginger's bones and avoid the pleasantries.

Before either man knew what was taking place, they were wrapped in each other's strong arms, sharing a deep, passionate kiss. As their wet tongues darted in and out of their mouths, their poles grew rock-hard. With Cassius being on top, he slow grinded his hips on Ginger's female-like shape. Groping, sucking, licking, biting, tugging, and finally, raw dick fucking until the sun was about to come up, they were both in heaven. Pastor Cassius Street felt he had made some sort of a twisted, yet very secret love connection. While Ginger, on the other hand, was convinced his new lover would gladly sign the lease to Me-Ma's house back over to him and his sisters—where it rightfully belonged. After all, Ginger wasn't about to waste a perfectly good opportunity to be the hero in their die-hard situation.

CHAPTER ELEVEN

"*Rhythm is a dancer, I need a companion. Girl, I guess that must be you. Body like the summer, fucking like no other. Don't you tell 'em what we do. Don't tell 'em . . .*"

"All right, y'all, show this lovely young lady some love. Bless her with some of that dough you holding onto like you gonna make some cookies tomorrow. Make it rain and show some appreciation for one of the hardest-working females under this roof. The one we call Miss Tiffany." The DJ was still doing what he did trying to coax and encourage the patrons of the strip club to tip. "All right, now, I see two real niggas in the house showing out and showing the way." One man tucked a few twenties in Tiffany's garter belt and returned to his seat where he had a steak dinner waiting. Another man then got up from his table off to the side and whispered something into the dancer's ear. Tiffany smiled, then nodded her head.

"Hey, Chase, what did you tell her?"

"Nothing much. I just told her I was a friend of Ghostman's and wanted to turn her onto something deep. I ain't know how she was gonna react, but I took a chance."

"Damn, guy. And it had her cheesing like that? I mean, damn!"

"Hell, yeah, Jakes. I guess dead or alive, that man's name rings bells."

"Yeah, I guess so."

"Well, she gonna come sit with us as soon as she comes off the stage and goes to the bathroom. Hopefully we can get her to talk."

After returning from pretending he was some sort of Big Willy, the random man brushed by Bunny who was standing a foot or so away from his table. Being the true trick that he was, he, of course asked the fully clothed beauty to join him for a drink while he ate his meal. Getting no response from a silent Bunny who seemed to be in deep thought, he shrugged his shoulder, knowing there were plenty other females up in that spot that were desperate for his attention, and he had more than enough dollars to spread around. "Hey, miss, you forgot to bring me a knife," he caught the apron-wearing waitress before she breezed by to take another order. Putting his attention back on Tiffany, who'd just gathered her tips off the floor of the stage, he saw she was making her way down. Before he could get a chance to signal for the sweaty stripper to come give him a lap dance, the too-uppity-and-arrogant-to-even-speak Bunny had taken a few steps over, unknowingly blocking his view. At that point, he decided to get two other girls to tag team him.

Tiffany was making the best out of an extremely slow night. As she thought, there was no real ballin'-type money circulating. The fact another one of the dancers was having a birthday party at the club meant nothing; it was still whack as fuck on the tip-getting situation. Just as the final song was starting to end on her set, the thirsty headliner was blessed with a few dollars from one man, followed by some uplifting news from the next who approached her. *Dang, I hope this is one of*

*them funny-style guys from out of town that used to be
plugged with Ghostman. Maybe he remembers me from
being with that dead crazy motherfucker and wants to
spend some of that drug money on a sista. I showl in
the hell hope so 'cause I could use a come up right about
now. Maybe I can set him and his straitlaced homeboy
sitting over there stupid asses up too. They dressed like
some dorks, so I know they ain't gonna be on that for
real for real gangster tip. They probably just gonna give
that shit up, no questions asked!* Thinking nothing but
positive thoughts, Tiffany took her last swing around the
brass pole. Running her fingers through her expensive
weave, she then slid down as seductively as possible.
Making sure all the men in the club could get a generous
view of her G-string-clad ass, she stuck it out, then up in
the air as she crawled around the lighted stage. Having
collected all her tips, Tiffany grabbed her bikini top that
was discarded to the side and pressed it up to her full
double-D breasts. No sooner than her seven-inch patent
leather skinny heel stiletto touched the carpeted floor,
Tiffany signaled to the man she hoped to get some real
Ghostman-type money out of later that she'd be right
back in a few. She even solidified the deal by blowing him
a kiss and letting them know it was on.

Bunny was growing sick to her stomach watching
Tiffany. She wanted to throw up. As the minutes dragged
by, she wanted to scream and yell. It was taking everything in her inner soul not to run up on that tramp
and snatch the female bald. The way she was feeling,
Bunny wanted to rip every single strand of weave out of
Tiffany's head, then spit directly in her face. Here, this
funky-mouth thang was twirling around the stage acting
as if shit was all good. She was climbing the pole, hanging

upside down, and doing tricks. This belly-rolling bitch was making tips here and there and smiling; grinning all up in niggas' faces. Her no-good ass was living life with no worries or guilt over getting Spoe and Tariq murdered. Bunny trembled. Her heart raced, and her anger increased. Her fingers felt as if they were throbbing, and her legs tensed up. She was only a few yards away from the one person left alive that could tell her how and why Spoe was gone. Tiffany was the reason Bunny slept alone every night, and the reason she had to commit a federal offense and rob a freaking bank. This two-bit stripper had single-handedly made Bunny turn from living the life to possibly doing life if she and her sisters ever got found out. She had to question this wannabe Beyoncé broad. There was no other way around Bunny living any part of a normal life if she didn't get some direct answers from Tiffany . . . and then the gleeful satisfaction of killing her afterward.

What in the fuck! Why is this man trying to speak to me after he just tipped that skank? As if I even look like I'm on the same level as her. Like I'm that damn desperate to want to have a drink with his creepy ass, let alone sit the hell across from him and watch his ugly self eat. Where the fuck they do that at? Certainly not here and definitely not with me. Seething with fury, Bunny was way past homicidal, to say the least. If there was no other person in life she detested, wanting to see dead, it was this diseased twat whore. Bunny coldly eye fucked the rear head of another man that felt compelled by his dick head to tip Tiffany.

Hurry the fuck up, music! Hurry up! Bunny counted down the seconds until the song playing would be over and she and Tiffany could be face-to-face. *"Rhythm is a dancer, I need a companion. Girl, I guess that must be you. Body like the summer, fucking like no other. Don't*

*you tell 'em what we do. Don't tell 'em. Don't tell 'em. You
don't even. Don't tell 'em. You don't even."* Then, just like
that, the song ended. Watching her soon-to-be victim
like a hawk, she moved over a small bit, making sure
she didn't lose sight of her mark in the dimness of the
club. Bunny's adrenalin jumped when Tiffany stepped off
the stage. She knew it was go time when the sneaky ho
headed toward the rear of the club. With ill intentions,
Bunny Banks followed.

"Hey, Tiffany, you was throwing down up there," one
of the dancers remarked, coming out of the dressing
room. "You be making all the money up in this mug."

"Whatever, girl," she nonchalantly replied, waving the
female off. "Go on out there and you'll see what's really
good."

Bunny fell back a little bit while ear hustling on the sly.
Just hearing the annoying sound of Tiffany's arrogant
voice made her want to just gut the female right there
in the dark hallway—no questions asked. A few feet
later, much to Bunny's advantage, Tiffany went into the
women's bathroom. *Good. I don't have to confront her in
front of the rest of these thirsty bitches.*

Going into one of the empty stalls, Tiffany unrolled an
enormous amount of tissue to wipe the squat-splattered
seat dry. Rudely tossing the tissue on the floor, she tore
off more, lining the seat before sitting down. After peeing,
the seasoned stripper opened her candy-apple red satin
pull string bag. Staring down at what couldn't be any more
than a few hundred dollars at best, she frowned at her
night's take. "I should just call it a night. Maybe ole boy
and his friend got some better shit popping than this slow
motherfucker," Tiffany mumbled out loud as she stood to
wipe herself. Using the sole of her shiny patent leather boot,
she flushed the toilet. Straightening out her tiny bikini
top, she then slid the flimsy latch to open the metal door.

Before the arrogant dancer knew what was happening, she had been socked in the facc. She saw bright blue and yellow lightning flashes. She wanted to speak but was stunned and couldn't form the words. Dazed from the forceful unexpected blow, her knees grew weak. As she wobbled to stay on her feet, Tiffany leaned against the wall of the small stall. Still dizzy, she could scarcely make out what female had a sharp knife pressed against the upper side of her throat threatening to slice it open.

"If you wanna die sooner than later, then open your big fat mouth and scream." Bunny pressed the blade harder, coming close to puncturing Tiffany's skin. "I'm looking for a reason to just gut the shit out of you anyway! I swear to God, I'm looking for just one damn reason! Open that mouth and you gonna give me one."

Tiffany usually had a lot of mouth. Like a lot of bully bitches like her, she was all talk and not really about that fighting life. She could talk a good game and have other females buffaloed, but at the end of the day, she didn't want no real static. It wasn't in her DNA. Instead of trying to go ham and go for bad, Tiffany just nodded, showing no resistance.

"Do you remember me, ho? Do you?" Tiffany squinted her eyes, finally getting a good look at her infuriated attacker. Her face showed immediate signs of panic realizing who and what this ambush was truly about. "So I guess you *do* remember, huh, bitch? Spoe's girl. His fucking woman!" With the steak knife still lodged under Tiffany's neck, Bunny punched her twice in the side of her lower ribcage. "I need to ask you a few things. And trust, it's in your best interest to answer. You feel me?" Bunny shoved the knife deeper into Tiffany's skin, slicing through the top layer. "And if I even feel you lying, I ain't gonna hesitate to slice your ho-motherfucking-ass ear to ear."

Tiffany was beyond terrified. Praying for someone to come into the bathroom and save her from Spoe's revenge-seeking wifey, God failed to listen. She was on her own this time and had to either follow instructions or meet the same fate as Spoe, Tariq, and Ghostman. "Okay, okay, sis," she struggled to speak as she bargained for her life to be spared. "What is it? What do you need to know? I'll tell you everything. Please, just don't hurt me!"

Bunny was pissed. Beyond all the harm and turmoil this tramp had brought into her life, she had the nerve to call her "sis," like it was all good. "Listen, you foul bitch! You ain't my sister, and we freaking ain't cool. This is what exactly the fuck it is. Me asking your ho ass what happened to my man Spoe the night he got murdered, and you telling me. So run that fucking mouth, bitch— and nothing else. So where was Spoe when I got to that apartment, and why did you set my people up in the first damn place?"

"Spoe wasn't there. Just Tariq was. I swear to God."

"I know that much, dummy, so don't play with me."

"I'm not! I'm not!"

"All right then. I said, *where* in the fuck was Spoe at then? Please don't make me keep asking you the same damn shit over and over. You making me pissed!"

"Okay, okay, please! Wait! Wait! I'm about to tell you."

"Well, then, tell me and stop all that 'okay, please' crap you blowing out your fucking mouth. Where the fuck was my baby at? Where was Spoe, bitch?"

"Tariq said him and Spoe ran up in Dino's crib, and he came home and caught them."

"Dino?"

"Yeah, Dino."

"Bitch, who in the fuck is Dino?"

"A dude from up in NYC. I was fucking with him."

"What?" Bunny grew puzzled the more Tiffany tried to spin the tale of the deadly night. "Dino from NYC? Look, girl, ain't nobody got no time to be playing word games with you while you stall for time. I ain't trying to hear that dumb shit no more!"

Tiffany took a deep breath attempting to explain what she knew would only make the person holding a sharp blade to her throat angrier. "I told Tariq about this cat I know named Dino. He the head of some dudes named the Bloody Lions Posse."

"The Bloody Lions Posse?"

"Yeah . . . They from NYC."

"And . . .?" Bunny applied more pressure to her victim's neck to further stress the point she was serious.

"And I told Tariq he had a bunch of money at his house."

"Well, how the fuck Ghostman get involved in the bullshit?"

"Tariq and Spoe had hit a few of Ghostman's spots real heavy over the past month."

"So and . . .?"

"I mean, they hit them real, real hard. He wanted to catch up with them and get his money back. He was tired of taking losses."

Bunny thought back to the night she and Spoe made love after one of his and Tariq's biggest robberies ever. *That must've come from Ghostman.* Now some of what Tiffany was saying was starting to make some sense, but Bunny knew there was much more to the deadly story. "Okay, then, why you tell them to hit Dino? Why you set them up to do that shit?"

Tiffany was terrified what Bunny would do if she told her the rest of the story as she knew it. She knew it was ultimately by her hand that all the wheels got set in motion. Both Spoe and Tariq were dead by her decisions—the same decisions that were about to possibly have her pushing up daisies as well. "Ghostman said if they didn't have his money he was going to kill both of them. I knew Tariq wasn't gonna just hand him over all that money, so I turned him on to hit another lick so he wouldn't feel the total lost. Yeah, I did know I was gonna get paid off the top, but you know how it is, sis."

Bunny sucker punched her once more this time, making a kidney the body blow count. "What in the fuck did I tell your ass about calling me that? I ain't your damn sis! And naw, ho, I don't know how it is!"

Tiffany coughed up a small bit of mucus. Tears started to pour out both eyes as her knees grew even weaker. "I'm sorry! I'm sorry!"

"Fuck being sorry. You gonna mess around and be dead. Now like I said from jump, where was Spoe when I got there?" Bunny demanded, tired of the cat-and-mouse game Tiffany was playing. After slowing slicing the side of the girl's face and drawing blood, Tiffany knew she had to reveal the entire truth.

"Tariq said Dino and his crew chased both them down in the woods near his mansion. He said at one point Spoe went down. He said he didn't want to leave him like that, but Spoe told him to take the bags with the money and dope and just get the fuck on." Tiffany was breathing hard as she told the deadly tale. "Tariq said he got a few hundred yards away and heard a gunshot. He said ole boy had some dogs on his ass so he ran to the van he and Spoe left parked on the other side of the woods. That nigga claimed he drove around for about a good hour or so and Spoe never came out of the woods. He called me crying, saying he know Spoe was gone. After that, I told him to at least bring the money over to the apartment. He ain't know Ghostman was there."

"What? So what you telling me is Ghostman ain't kill Spoe?" Bunny was confused. Feeling like someone had let the air out of her emotions, she was almost broken down. The only thing that was keeping her strong was her taste for revenge.

"Naw, he ain't never even laid eyes on Spoe. If what Tariq said was true, Dino and his crew killed Spoe. That was the first time he ever saw Tariq. He'd just heard about both them and knew they was the stickup dudes that was hitting all his spots."

Bunny was infuriated. She couldn't believe what she was hearing. "So why in the fuck did y'all involve me? If Spoe wasn't there, and y'all had the money and drugs they'd stolen from Dino, then why call me? Huh? Why?"

Tiffany knew what she was about to say was gonna get her killed, but she had to roll the dice and take a chance. "Because Ghostman got greedy, and I told him you could get both Tariq's and Spoe's stash and bring it to us!"

"What?" Bunny hissed with undeniable rage. "So that asshole not only had Dino's shit, he made me bring the cash I needed to live off of too? Then had the nerve to come to my grandmother's repast and extort even more money from me?" Bunny was heated. After all, that was the true reason they'd robbed the bank in the first damn place, to repay that bastard.

"Yeah, but, but . . . If you wanna be mad at anybody, be pissed at Tariq's coward ass. I mean, he the one that called you that night, not me. I mean, shit, he and Spoe was stickup boys from off rip, you know that. They luck was gonna run out sooner or later anyway. They was gonna screw up and somebody was gonna end up killing they asses either way. Sis, you know that's part of the game! You know how we do."

That was the last thing Bunny wanted to hear and the last thing Tiffany would say. *Kill this rotten bitch and*

*just get it over with. Make her bleed the way Spoe had
to bleed. Make this ho feel the pain my baby probably
felt,* the voices in her head kept taunting, urging her to
take instant action. Karma had shown up and was about
to show out.

Using all her strength, Bunny stabbed the conniving
female multiple times in the rear of her skull. In and out
with the ease of a butcher slicing meat, she'd tasted her
mother and Lenny's blood earlier, so this was nothing.
Amused at Tiffany fighting to live to see another sunrise,
Bunny sadistically whispered into the dancer's ear to say
her final prayers, letting her lifeless body fall to the urine-
stained floor as she leaned close, slashing her victim's
throat. Tiffany's eyes were eerily wide open, but she was
no more.

Reaching over, removing the satin bag that lay by
Tiffany's side, Bunny didn't break a sweat. Untying the
string, she opened the bag. She removed Tiffany's cell
phone along with a crumbled up fifty-dollar bill. Taking
the rest of the cash out, she disrespectfully tossed it onto
Tiffany's face. Callously, Bunny proceeded to mash some
of the filthy currency into the self-proclaimed queen of
the strip club's mouth. "Here the hell you go! You mon-
ey-hungry bitch! Live off this shit in fucking hell!" After
that brutal one-sided exchange of rage, Bunny snatched
the girl's expensive gold and huge diamond-encrusted
monogramed tennis bracelet off her floppy wrist. Not
wanting to half step, Bunny then, showing no pity for
the deceased, yanked down both of Tiffany's one-carat
diamond screw back stud earrings, splitting both lobes.
"Thanks, trick. I know Tariq, Ghostman, that dude Dino
or some other dim-witted cat whose dick you was sucking
sponsored this shit . . . so easy come, easy the fuck go. It's
mine now!"

Done doing the deed, Bunny left the small stall. Without an inch of remorse for the slaying or fear of getting caught, she nonchalantly walked over to the sink. Not wanting to have sweaty and bloody palms, she thoroughly washed her hands. Coldly, Bunny smiled as she looked into the mirror admiring herself and who she was. *Perfect as always. Not a hair out of place. Without a doubt, I'm that bitch!*

Going back into the main area of the noisy club, Bunny had no idea whatsoever that her sister's man, Detective Chase Dugan, was sitting only a few yards away. Even if she did know his police ass was in the house, that still wouldn't have halted her plan of the assassination of the cocky stripper. With pride in her stride, she casually walked out the front doors feeling almost whole again. Bunny was now satisfied that Tiffany got what was coming to her for being such a slimeball. The grubby trick had a bad habit of setting paid Negros up, so now she got a little payback. Like Tiffany said when she tried to go momentarily hard, it was all part of the game. Now Bunny would focus on tracking this dude Dino down just like she'd done Tiffany. She now had tunnel vision for making him pay for his sins; him and his boys. They'd taken Spoe from her, now they had to repay that debt in full. Dino and the entire Bloody Lions Posse would wish they were back in NYC when she was done. *In time, baby, I promise I will get them all!*

After the valet pulled Bunny's car up and handed her the keys, she smiled. With pride, she blessed him yet again. This time, with a crumbled up fifty-dollar bill. Working for tips, he would never forget her and her generosity that night.

CHAPTER TWELVE

Detective Dugan and Officer Jakes finished sipping on their juices while watching a few more females shake their asses and swing from the pole. Looking down at his watch, Jakes finally made mention that it didn't seem as if the girl Tiffany was coming back to sit with them.

"I mean, really, man, how long does it take to go to the bathroom? I done took a full-on dump in less time."

"Maybe she's in the dressing room changing outfits or something. You know how vain these dancers are, especially one as fine as that one is. Maybe she's somewhere giving lap dances or something."

"You think?" Jakes gave Chase the "nigga please" side eye. "It's been a mighty long damn time, and we still out here waiting like some lames."

"Naw, you might just be right, guy. That girl might be slicker than I thought. Maybe I scared her off. I hope not, because she has the potential to be the link we need to close these cases out once and for all."

Just as the two police were exchanging their spate speculations of what was taking Tiffany so long, one of the other dancers ran out the side of the stage as if there was someone or something chasing her. Her arms were flinging from side to side and she called out to Jesus to help her repeatedly. With the piercing sounds of her screaming exceeding the volume of the music blasting through the speakers, all eyes were on her. Through the tears flowing and her painful sobbing, the officers of the law instinctively approached the growing crowd of staff and other patrons to see what all the commotion was about. In a matter of seconds, a tidal wave of gossip swept throughout the club. The distraught dancer tragically had discovered one of her own dead in bathroom stall with her neck sliced wide open.

"I-I-I—" she stuttered as the tears continued to pour out from her red eyes. "I went in there to pee and check my makeup because the dressing room was so crowded, and there was blood on the floor. It was like someone spilled something. It was just running from the stall to the drain. I ain't know what it was at first," she started screaming again as she relived what she'd just seen. "I seen somebody's legs and body when I looked under the door. I tried to push it open, and at first, it was kinda stuck. Then I used my hip and peeked in. It was-it was-it was—" Now damn near hysterical, the stripper was putting on a performance worthy of winning an Academy Award. "It was Tiffany lying on the floor! It was her—Tiffany! Our Tiffany! Oh my God! Her neck was bleeding. It was open—like a big hole open; like something tried to tear her neck from her body! I saw it! I saw it! Her eyes was wide open like she was looking at me or something. There was blood everywhere. Then she had a lot of money stuffed in her mouth. Well, not a lot, but some." The dancer continued with her hysterics, putting on the ultimate performance.

Detective Dugan and Officer Jakes wasted no more time. Immediately, they made the announcement that they were police and for everyone to step back. After practically fighting to clear everyone out of the women's bathroom, they saw firsthand that the wild story the stripper was claiming she'd seen was indeed true. The club headliner Tiffany they were waiting to question about the bank robberies and several murders had been murdered herself . . . only a few yards from where they were sitting nursing two glasses of fruit juice. Without hesitation, the detective called the crime in. Dugan and Officer Jakes then secured the murder scene, trying to preserve any evidence that hadn't already been destroyed or compromised by the stunned dancers, staff, and nosy patrons that all had their cell phones in hand, cruelly recording the unfortunate occurrence.

Finally clearing the scene of all patrons and dancers, Detective Dungan turned to Officer Jakes. "How in the world are we going to explain this shit when we were only feet away? This is not going to be good."

"Well, all we can do now is prepare for our asses being ripped wide open! Shit!"

News cameras and reporters were posted outside Treat's Gentlemen's Club. As the early-morning crowds of gawkers gathered, so did the rumors of what exactly had taken place. Throughout the years the adult entertainment establishment was open, there had been more than several shootings outside the perimeter. And more than their fair share of physical altercations inside the dwelling. But this was the first time the rambunctious club had experienced this type of violent crime; a heinous murder in the bathroom.

As the owner and staff were getting questioned, more than close to seventy-five to a hundred patrons had retreated from the club to either avoid contact with the law, having their faces shown on television, or run the risk of their girlfriends, spouses, or significant others finding out where they'd been all evening. This had not been overlooked by the police. Of course, one of them was possibly the killer, but with all the club's security cameras broken, identifying any or all of them would be an almost impossible feat.

"So, you telling me you two knuckleheads were in here when this girl was murdered? What in the hell y'all want me to tell the mayor? Y'all want me to tell him two of my top men I got working on the high-profile bank robberies got their heads stuck so far up in their asses they can't speculate not one person that could've sliced her damn neck wide open like that?" The chief of police was livid. The mayor was up for reelection and was trying his best to get a strong-arm handle on the spike in violent crimes throughout the city. The more disturbed and angrier the mayor got, the more pressure he applied to his handpicked appointed chief of police. Of course, shit rolled downhill, so Detective Dugan and Officer Jakes were facing a full-blown shit storm of it.

"Chief, hold up. Hear me out," the detective bargained, trying to explain. "We were here and did indeed speak to the victim. She said she was going to the bathroom and would return. I mean, we sat right here and waited. There was no way we could have known this was going to happen."

"Like I said, you two sat a few yards away while that girl was being murdered. *My* freaking policemen! On *my* watch! Damn! Right in there," he disappointedly pointed over toward the roped off bathroom. "First, the string of robberies. Then all these dead bodies washing up on shore. My men just got called out to the scene of two more. These two were stabbed up and set on fire."

Detective Dugan was tired of getting chewed out for trying to do his job and decided to speak out to clear his name, no matter what the outcome. "Okay, Chief, look. She said she was going to the bathroom. I mean, what did you want us to do? Follow her in there and watch her do whatever women do in there? The walls ain't made of glass. How in the hell could we see what was going down? You know like I do, it only takes one second to kill someone if you really want to. Just like everybody else that we done interviewed, we didn't see or hear anything either. There was nothing to indicate something of that nature was going to happen."

The chief wanted to yell and berate his officers further, but unfortunately, he had to step outside and deal with the reporters that were getting small bits and pieces of conflicting information regarding the crime. He knew they were trying to go live with their early news program scheduling, so he felt it best to appease them. "Hey, just do what you need to do to get this bullshit under control! All our damn jobs depend on it! And, Detective, you might as well get ready and get yourself all pretty for these damn cameras outside. If I gotta face this firing squad, you're coming with me!"

CHAPTER THIRTEEN

Ginger glanced over at the black leather couch and licked his lips. Pastor Street was just where he'd left him after their last wild go-around; stretched out butt-asshole naked. After all the "special attention" he'd shown the pastor, he finally got the favor returned; more than once or twice. Slowly reaching for his cell, he placed the volume on silent. After making sure the flash was off, Ginger started taking picture after picture of the religious sleeping beauty. Placing the risqué photos in the same file as the scandalous video Bunny had taken at Me-Ma's and sent to him, Ginger smirked with satisfaction. He knew these pictures might come in handy one day, but hoped there would be no need. Placing his cell back in his blue jean pocket, Ginger crawled his perfect female-shaped body over toward the couch. Wanting to get one more taste of Cassius Street's juices before the sun came all the way up, Ginger took all of him in his mouth. As he eagerly sucked and slurped to the tune of the birds starting to chirp outside the church's window, the man of God woke up stiff as a board, and ready to go a few more rounds. With his right hand on the rear of Ginger's head and the left unknowingly on top of a Bible, Pastor Street jerked with pleasure, quickly shooting his early-morning load off into Ginger's warm, moist mouth.

"Hey, you. Good morning," Cassius spoke with none of the shame or bashfulness he had the night before. They'd been pleasuring each other for hours on end, so all the strict formalities were a thing of the past.

Ginger happily swallowed the thick substance before speaking. "Hey, yourself. How did you sleep?"

"Like a baby."

"Yeah, me too."

"Hey, what time is it?" Cassius heard the birds and looked at his watch. He had morning-prayer offerings scheduled. And even though he'd enjoyed the night he and Ginger shared, the money-greedy preacher didn't want to miss out on his extra pocket money. With clothes to get out to the cleaners, he had plans of using this morning's collected funds to pay the tab.

"It's time for me to be getting up, huh?"

"Well . . . it's just that . . ."

Ginger knew what that meant and had no problem with taking the walk of shame. Slipping on his jeans, then his shoes, he bent over pecking the pastor on his bare chest. "Soooo, listen, Cassius. Before I be out, we need to chop it up."

"About?"

"About that deed Me-Ma left to you in her will."

"The deed?"

"Yes, silly Negro, yes, the deed. The deed to the house that belongs to me and my sisters!"

Pastor Street stood to his feet. Grabbing for his clothes that were scattered all about the church office, he looked confused. "I'm sorry, Ginger, but what about the deed?"

"Well, are you going to give us back our damn house or what?" Ginger caught an immediate attitude, shifting all his weight onto one hip. "I know you don't think it's yours to keep. Do you?"

"No, Ginger, I don't think it's mine to keep."

"You damn straight it's not yours!"

"Yes, it belongs to the church. That's the way your grandmother wanted it to be, and shouldn't we honor and respect her wishes?"

"What the fuck you trying to say?"

"Like I told you and your sisters, if you all would like to bid on the house, I definitely don't have a problem with that. I told all four of you this is not personal; it's strictly business."

Ginger was irate. Wanting to destroy everything in the small office, he chilled the best he possibly could. "Oh, so you think it's that easy to gank the Banks sisters? You think we gonna fold just like that, huh? It's going to be that easy, huh?"

Pastor Street sensed the extreme rage in Ginger's mannerisms and took a few steps backward in case he had to retreat. "So was getting the deed back what this was about—me and you? I mean, was that the plan; the big picture? If so, thank you, but no, thank you!"

"It wasn't at first, but if you think you can just take back all that fucking and sucking I done did, you sadly mistaken. But since you feeling like it's whatever, then, let it be. Let it motherfucking ride! I'm about to be all up in my zone!" Ginger placed his hands on his hips and rolled his neck. It was obvious the lustful nature shared last night between the two men had changed drastically. Ginger was not with the games anymore; from anyone. He'd watched Bunny kill his mother and didn't shed a single tear, so as far as he was concerned, wasn't no man, woman, or beast gonna move him. He was unbreakable.

"Wait one minute. First, are you threatening me? Second, didn't you want it too?" Pastor Street then calmly asked like he was some sort of a superhero eyeballing the villain. "Because if you are—"

"Naw, guy, I don't do threats, but man to man, you might wanna tighten that slick tone of yours up. I might dress like a female, but please don't try me! I'm not only good with my mouth but with my hands as well."

"Once again, Ginger, what are you saying? Please just spit it out! I'm not good with all these word and mind games!"

"Nigga, please, fall all the way back. You're the king, or should I say the low-key flaming queen of master fucking manipulation."

"What?" the pastor asked as if what Ginger was saying had no great merit.

"You heard me, chump. I mean, that's how you swindled our grandmother in the first place, ain't it? With that velvet tongue you had buried deep in my asshole last night!"

"Excuse me," he twisted his face not believing how Ginger had flipped in a mere matter of minutes. "I don't take anything from anyone. Now, if these women want to all bless me with gifts of all sorts, who am I to turn down what God has for me? I never asked your grandmother to give the church anything. She did that all on her own."

Ginger headed for the door and evilly giggled before leaving. "Let's just say, Pastor Good-Dick-Sucking-Street, you better stay prayed up fucking with me and mines! You playing like you all rough and tough, but let's be clear . . . Me and my sisters are about that life! By the way, I hope Me-Ma is looking down on you so you better prepare yourself for what's coming your way, Pastor Low-Dick-Loving-Street."

CHAPTER FOURTEEN

For the first time in over a week, Simone actually had a good night's sleep. Unlike her siblings, she woke up in her own bed. Tallhya was sedated at the mental hospital. Ginger had gone ho hopping with Pastor Street, and Bunny had checked into a cheap hotel off the interstate to clear her mind. Even though she'd suffered through numerous heartaches, trials, and tribulations recently, she felt as if things might be looking up for her.

The fact that she'd witnessed her mother being killed the day before by her sister in the very house she had slept in meant nothing. Simone was good with it. Fixing herself a strong cup of coffee, she tied the belt on her robe. After yawning, she lazily slid her house shoes across the kitchen floor. Going into the living room, Simone placed her mug on the sofa table. Ready to catch the early-morning newscast, she plopped down on the couch. As she clicked the remote channel surfing, Simone finally came to the *Good Morning, Richmond* program. Waiting anxiously for the cheerful anchors to finish with the first weather and traffic report of the broadcast, Simone watched the breaking news banner flash across the thirty-two inch flat screen. Praying she and Ginger's deadly secret by the James River hadn't been immediately discovered, she bit at the side of her fingernails. God had blessed her to get away with so much shenanigans as of recently, she knew it was only a matter of time before the devil himself stepped in and intercepted her good luck.

To Simone's relief, the top story of the morning started with an overnight fatal shooting at a strip club. Taking a small sip of her coffee she turned up the volume.

"*Accurate reports are hard to come by at this time; however, from what we can gather, it was indeed a homicide that took place in the late hours of the night in the building behind me. The few witnesses that were willing to speak to us off camera say that it was a little after midnight when the victim, now identified as Tiffany K. Ross, age twenty-five, a dancer at Treat's Gentlemen's Club, was last seen exiting the stage. Another employee stated she'd spoken to her briefly before she went inside the bathroom. Our sources also tell us that the bathroom, located a few yards from the main area of the adult entertainment establishment, was the place where she was murdered. Apparently, there was some sort of altercation between her and the assailant. Not yet able to identify the perpetrator, the authorities are looking for some assistance from some of the many patrons that were inside the club at the time when the brutal crime was committed. Earlier, we spoke to the chief of police and Detective Chase Dugan who we are more than familiar with from the dual bank robberies that took place last week.*"

"*Yes, it is true. It was indeed a homicide that took place tonight,*" the chief confirmed.

"*Well, can you maybe tell our viewing audience how the victim was killed? Maybe the circumstances?*"

"*Well, I, of course, can't give you the particulars of the case as we are just in the beginning stages; however, I can tell you the victim's neck was cut.*"

"*Cut?*"

"*Yes, our victim's neck was slashed.*"

"Well, can you give me a description of the suspect you guys are looking for that committed such an awful, horrific act? I mean, is there anything our viewers should be on the lookout for; a license plate number or something?"

The chief had his fill of being in the bright lights of the camera. Without hesitation, he placed his hand on the detective's shoulder. *"I'm quite sure you know Detective Chase Dugan. He can answer any other questions you may have, but please make them brief. We all have work to do. Thank you for your cooperation."*

Like a small deer caught in the headlights, the detective was slow and cautious with every response he gave the reporters. When he was finished, they had enough to go live, yet not enough pertinent information to ridicule the fact he and his fellow officer were actually on the premises when the murder of Tiffany Ross took place.

"Wow, Chase. You looking so damn good in that Polo shirt and jeans. And those muscles in your arms . . ." Simone was speaking to the television screen as if her detective beau could really hear her impromptu compliments. Without question, Simone was saddened by the reported details concerning the heinous murder. The fact some seemingly innocent female had been brutally killed by having her throat slashed was more disturbing to her than Bunny slicing their mother and Lenny from foot to 'fro. Simone had no worldly idea that the dead dancer had died by the same hands as those two. Nevertheless, she still kept a keen eye on the television just in case they had an additional two discarded body counts to increase the James River's dumping ground count. Enduring what seemed like the longest commercial filled the first eleven minutes of the news, then Simone exhaled. She was sure that if the bodies had been found, it would've made at least the second or third top story. But now, they were covering the weather yet once again. "I might need to call Chase and at least see if he knows or heard anything. I can't be living on pins and needles like this. I can't be caught off guard."

Moments before Simone placed the call, Ginger bolted through the front door hotter than fish grease. Slamming the door with the superstrength of three men, Ginger wasted no time in filling Simone in on the details of his night. "This fool think I'm some sort of a joke; we are some jokes."

"Wait a minute. Hold up," Simone put both hands in the air. "Slow down. I'm confused."

Ginger had to catch his breath. Known to be the flamboyant drama queen of the family, he knew he had tendencies to talk faster than average folk could comprehend. "Look, after that dick-stroker-in-disguise called me last night, I shot right over there."

"Over where?"

"The church."

"Nooo . . . not the church." Simone's eyes bucked as she giggled.

"Yesss . . . bitch, yesss. The motherfucking church. You heard what I said," Ginger replied with no shame or guilt in his voice for violating the house of God.

"Oh my."

"Yeah, well, when a bitch got there, you know it was all good my way. You know good and damn well I wasn't leaving out of the house any time after ten on a damn Friday night on no dry dick run. If I put my shoes on these pretty, manicured feet and waste my gas, high as that bullshit is, it was gonna be some serious fucking and sucking going on. And I mean *serious!*"

Simone was all in listening to Ginger talk that talk. Never being one to live on the edge, over the years, she'd grown accustomed to live vicariously through her sister's wild-spirited existences. "Please tell me you didn't, Ginger. Please!"

Ginger cracked a smile realizing Simone was being a prude of sorts. "I had that queen bent over begging for more of this bronze pole I was cursed being born with. Then this morning, he had the nerve to get tough toned with me."

"What?"

"Yeah, talking about he wasn't gonna sign over the deed to this house to me."

"Hold up, did he ever say he was?" Simone sat up on the edge of the couch interested in the answer Pastor Street gave.

"Naw, but I don't give a sweet shit about what he actually said or thought."

"Oh, wow!"

"Oh, wow, nothing, Simone. I know his undercover ass ain't think I was giving up all this meat for nothing. There's a price to pay for everything, and I do mean everything."

"I guess so," she giggled.

"Shidd, you guessed right. I mean, sis, he tried to talk all slick, but trust, I got something real deep for that ass. But forget all that right now." Ginger kicked off his shoes and fell back onto Me-Ma's favorite chair to catch his breath. "What in the hell your ass doing up all early on a Saturday morning?"

Simone informed Ginger that she'd wanted to watch the first news report of the day to see if they'd found Deidra and Lenny yet. "I didn't see anything about what we did, but I did see some girl got her throat slashed down at the strip club Spoe's boy Tariq used to hang out at."

"Treat's?"

"Yeah, that's it. And guess who they interviewed?"

"Let me damn guess; your Inspector Gadget boy-friend?" Ginger turned up his lip while rubbing on his feet.

Simone laughed at the comparison. "Yup, Chase's fine ass. He said one of the dancers named Tiffany got her head damn near cut off her body."

"Tiffany!" Ginger leaped to her feet almost kicking over the sofa table. "Did you say a dancer down at that piece-of-shit club? You mean that son of a bitch named Tiffany?"

"Yeah, I think so. Why?"

"Fuck all the whys right about now. Have you spoken to Bunny?"

"Bunny? Naw, not since she left here. I tried calling her again late last night, but I still got the voice mail."

"Shit!"

"Shit, what? What's wrong?"

"Come on, Simone. I know your memory ain't that bad. You know that's the damn female that Bunny said set Spoe and Tariq up, don't you? She said her name was Tiffany, and the ignorant bitch danced at that club. We need to find out where Bunny at. Fast and in a hurry!"

Simone sat motionless. As she replayed the conversation she and Bunny had, it soon came back to her that Ginger was correct. The girl's name was Tiffany, and she was one of the headliners at Treat's Gentlemen's Club. Without hesitation, she ran to the stairs. Sprinting up the stairs and back, she returned with her cell phone in hand. Pulling up Bunny's name, she hit Talk. One short ring and her call was directly sent to voice mail. This time was different than the others because Simone was not able to leave a message since the box was filled to capacity. "I can't even leave a damn message for her ass. We need to go over to her house, like now!"

***

As Ginger drove to Bunny's condo, Simone called Chase in hopes of obtaining information relating to the bodies and Bunny's disappearing ass.

"Good morning."

"Hey, sunshine. Good morning to you also. How did you sleep?"

"I slept well. I just called to tell you that you looked very handsome on the news this morning."

"Wow, you saw that, huh?"

"Yeah, why you say it like that? You looked good to me . . . considering the circumstances."

"Yeah, some dancer messed around and got killed; a real messy scene. But I know you don't wanna hear about all that drama."

He had no idea that was indeed all Simone wanted to hear about. Truth be told, that was the nature of the call in the first place . . . to fish for information not only about the murder at the club and if they had any suspects, but if he'd heard of anymore deceased bodies turning up at the river. "Not really, but I feel so sorry for that girl and her family. I hope you guys find out who did it."

"Yeah," Detective Dugan was distracted by someone coming into his office bringing him some files on yet a few more unsolved cases. "Sorry, Simone. What were you saying, sweetie?"

"Nothing much, Chase. I was just saying I hope you guys have the no-good man behind bars that hurt that girl last night. Doing her like that was a sin and a shame. I hope you locked him up and threw away the key."

"As much as I would love to say yeah, we got the scumbag off the street and get the chief and the damn mayor off my back, no dice. Not only do we have no leads, we don't even know if the killer is a man or a woman."

"A woman?"

"Yeah, Simone. You know, maybe one of the other girls was jealous of the victim's beauty or something." Chase was strangely enchanted by the dead girl Tiffany's perfect angelic face and seductive voice.

"Oh, so you think she was beautiful, huh?" Simone quizzed with envy almost forgetting the reason for the call. "I guess I should be kinda glad you dating me and only me, right?"

Chase smiled, feeling like the female he was so crazy about was also into him the same way as well. "Girl, you know it's no chick in the world I think is more flyer than you."

"Oh, okay, then," Simone laughed getting back on track as Ginger gave her the side eye. "Well, what else is going on? When are we going on another date? You owe me a steak dinner, or did you forget?"

"It's coming, I promise. Just as soon as I think we have one thing under control, though, some other mess pops up. First, the dancer getting killed last night while me and my partner were down at the club, then the two damn burned bodies by the riverbank."

"Down at the club? Two burned bodies? What?" she suspiciously repeated, shocked to hear both admissions. Playing the dumb role, she continued to dry pump him for even more information. "You were at the club last night other than investigating that someone burned up two people? Yeah, Chase, your life is way too busy for me and complicated."

"Naw, sweetie, it's not. I'll tell you what. Can you meet me today for a late lunch? I promise I'll be on time and not let anything stand in our way."

Not wanting to miss out on an opportunity to have a face-to-face with the man who was ultimately holding her and her siblings' freedom, unknowing, in his hands, Simone immediately replied yes before ending their conversation. Turning her attention back to Ginger, she informed him of the details of what Chase had said. "We're gonna have a late lunch. That way, I can really read his face and con the true four-one-one outta his ass!"

Seconds before they pulled into the empty driveway of Bunny's condo, Simone's cell phone rang. Automatically assuming it was Chase forgetting to tell her something, she answered without even looking at the screen. "Don't tell me you're cancelling on me. It only took all of what—two minutes?"

"Yes, hello. Is this Miss Simone Banks?"

"Umm . . . yes, it is," Simone removed her cell from her ear taking a quick look at the screen. Seeing a 1-800 number, she was still at a loss of who it was. "I'm sorry, but who's calling?"

"Yes, this is Capital Health Insurance Company. We're calling on behalf of Tallhya Banks-Walker and the facility she's currently admitted in. You are listed on the admission record as the main contact person."

"Yes, that's right. Is my sister okay?"

"Oh, she's fine as she can be. But we have a problem with billing."

"A problem? What kind of problem?"

"It seems that Walter Walker, listed as her spouse, recently cancelled her health insurance, so we need some other type of payment arrangements to be made by six o'clock this evening or she will be discharged."

"He did *what?*" Simone yelled, causing Ginger to stop from getting out of the parked car. *That low-down son of a bitch! I'm going to personally cut his throat!*

After confirming what her soon-to-be former brother-in-law had done, Simone filled in Ginger. Deciding one day soon Walter would be on their "list" of no-good motherfuckers who went against the grain of the Banks sisters that had to be dealt with, they smiled.

Luckily, Tallhya had taken the monthly payout of her lottery windfall and could easily cover her own medical bills when her next stipend was paid. For the time being, Simone assured the caller she'd be in the office by the end of the day with a check to cover her sister's expenses for the next week or so. Now totally disgusted or confused with most of the men they'd encountered over the past month, with the exception of Detective Dugan, Simone grimaced.

Walking up to Bunny's condo, she then motioned for Ginger to be quiet as they pressed their ears to the door. After hearing no movement or noise inside, Simone retrieved the spare key from the spot Bunny always hid it in. In a matter of seconds, she and Ginger were inside of the expensively decorated condo.

"Okay, now, this bullshit is creepy as a motherfucker. First, the bitch don't answer none of our calls. Then her car ain't here, and now this! What the hell *is* this?" Ginger snatched all three of the letters off of the dresser in Bunny's bedroom. Ripping the envelope open that had his name boldly written across the front, the reason for Bunny's absence became evident.

By the time Simone was finish reading her handwritten preconfession note of sorts, she knew they had to find Bunny as soon as possible. She'd said she was going to make Tiffany pay for what she'd done to Spoe and Tariq. And by all accounts of the tragic events that unfolded the night before at Treat's Gentlemen's Club, Bunny had kept her murderous word. Now they had to find their seemingly disturbed sister and save her from herself. Like the final sentence in the note read, by her own hand she'd be with Spoe, dancing in heaven, before she'd spend one night locked up in the hell that was prison.

CHAPTER FIFTEEN

Dino woke up with a new go-getter attitude and lease on life. Knowing he was a true hustler, he never missed a beat. Convinced he could double up and financially rebound from the major lost he suffered at the hands of Spoe and his mystery partner, he lit a blunt, blowing smoke up in the air. Tying his thick, waist-length dreads in a ponytail, he felt the energy of the day in his bones. He'd made things as right as he could with his connect. He had no choice if he and his boys wanted to continue running the narcotic-plagued neighborhoods they were holding down.

Having made several trips up to New York for face-to-face meetings with the main plug, Dino had a lot of explaining to do. Thankfully, the ruthless and rotten leader of the Bloody Lions Posse finally reassured the higher-ups the drug pipeline he'd worked almost a good year and three months on was back secure. He made his foreign investors see that it was only by sheer luck the men that'd infiltrated his home were able to get away with that much product and cash. Showing them plans of not only a new high-tech security system in place, but pictures of one of the culprits, Spoe, being half-eaten by the dogs, they finally were satisfied. Leaving Spanish Harlem with the confidence of the bosses he needed to make money, Dino vowed to never let anyone—man, woman, cat, or dog—get close enough again to know where his stash was.

Now, in less than two hours, the bloodthirsty drug merchant would accept delivery on a new drug package. That blessing from the dope gods would put him not only a little bit back in the game, but all the way back on his feet as well. Considering it was the day of his big pre-birthday bash at Club You Know, this come up was right on time. He reached for his phone and dialed the party promoter to ensure that there would be no surprises.

"Yeah, man, you guys got the bottles ready for me or what? I'm not bullshitting around tonight. We trying to turn the hell up in that motherfucker! I need to let this entire city know me and my posse still standing strong and ain't about to fall short no time soon!"

"Of course, Dino. You know we about our business down here at the club. For real, for real. Now, have we ever let you or your people down? I don't think so," the party promoter reassured one of his favorite and loyal customers. "When I say I got you, I got you. Besides VIP, which is practically sold out, we got the flyers posted all around the city; on Facebook and Instagram too."

Having confidence his party would be banging, Dino's mind was at ease. While getting dressed, the seasoned thug grabbed the oversized universal remote. With one click, he turned on not only the television, but the surround system as well. As the thunderous sounds kicked from the various speakers, he abruptly stopped dead in his tracks. He thought he was seeing wrong. He thought he was hearing wrong. It couldn't be, yet seemed as it was. *What in the entire fuck? Oh, hell, naw!* Paying close attention to the suit-and-tie-clad reporter on the midday newscast, Dino's mouth dropped open. The fact that the local strip club he and his boys would hang out at from time to time was the backdrop for a story was nothing. There was always some sort of petty crimes or minor disturbances taking place there. That bullshit was normal at a strip club. However, what was *not* normal was seeing the female's face—who was just calling him the night before like some sort of a stalker—plastered all across the sixty-five inch mounted flat screen.

Tiffany was everything that being a stripper, gold digger, opportunist, slut, ho, and bitch encompassed. She was all that . . . and more. Matter of fact, a master at her craft of hustling men out their cash. Now the always-down-for-whatever female could add another well-deserved title to her extensive ghetto résumé: murder victim. *Damn, I knew that bird was gonna get got one day, but shit . . . Now the sneaky tramp can't suck me off for a couple of dollars no more when a playa get a taste for some of that good head game she got—or rather had.*

Dino didn't know the circumstances behind Tiffany's demise but knew whoever took her out of the game had a good reason to do so. He had no real proof she was behind the deadly robbery at his house, yet, she was one of his suspects, so, fuck her was his mind-set. He was thrown off that she was dead, but that still didn't stop or put a damper on the fact his party was later that night. Dino was feeling himself and wasn't gonna let not no person—dead or alive—bring him down.

After finishing his breakfast blunt appetizer, he went down to the kitchen for the main course he smelled cooking. The infamous drug dealer's personal chef had come in extra early for his birthday and the potent weed had made him as hungry as five men combined.

Bunny spent the night at a cheap motel. Driving a few extra miles outside the city limits, she made sure she parked her vehicle near the rear of the building. Not knowing if someone would be able to shed any light on who committed Tiffany's heinous murder, she felt it best to be as low-key as possible. Not having any remorse for her brutal, but justified actions, Bunny had taken a shower. Feeling a sense of relief, she was totally relaxed. She'd ignored the constant back-to-back calls from Simone and Ginger. Bunny knew they could and would take care of the bloody situation she'd left behind in Me-Ma's basement. And if they couldn't, at this point in the game, she could care less. Bunny felt she had bigger fish to fry. Wrapped in a towel, she lay across the bed gazing up at the ceiling. As she held the pillow and thought of the same thing she'd been thinking about for the past couple of weeks, Bunny prayed Spoe was also thinking of her up in heaven.

Wiping a few tears out of the corner of each eye, Bunny rocked back and forth knowing she had to complete her deliberate task of revenge. Knowing what she now knew about Dino, there was no way in hell his mother wasn't gonna get the same call Spoe's lunatic mother had received. There was no way Dino's woman or jump off was gonna miss out on the feeling of heartache and pain she was enduring. No way in hell was Dino gonna enjoy walking these streets ever again without looking over his shoulder in fear. If Spoe was dead by Dino's hands, then he'd be dead by hers. Lenny's death meant nothing. Tiffany's also meant nothing, and killing her own mother in cold blood meant even less to Bunny. But sending Dino on his way was going to be like hitting the multistate jackpot. Bunny was as anxious to see him bleed out as she was on Christmas morning seeing a tree full of ribbon-wrapped toys.

Climbing out of bed, Bunny turned on the early news report to see if anything would be mentioned about the brazen crime she committed the night before. With wide-eyed anticipation, she sat on the edge of the bed. Not having to wait long, Bunny soon saw Treat's Gentlemen's

Club and her sister's beau Detective Chase Dugan taking center stage. Her hands shook and her heart raced as he was being asked question after question pertaining to the case. Attentively listening to every single word reported, Bunny smirked seeing Tiffany's picture then flash on the upper right-hand side of the television. Reading the word "victim" underneath the woman's name who set up Spoe to get murdered brought Bunny even more elation. *No suspects can be identified at this time, and no apparent motive in the slaughter. Hell, yeah!*

As Bunny Banks smiled, she reached over on the nightstand to grab Tiffany's stolen cell phone. Having turned off the GPS tracker before she even hit the corner the night before, Bunny was ready to get down to business. With an inner rage, she started the task of trying to track down Dino. Spoe's devoted wifey had no idea what his grimy Bloody Lions Posse ass looked like or where he lived. However, seeing how Tiffany and he were supposedly so damn close, Bunny knew she could find all the answers she wanted in the smartphone she was holding in her hands. Revenge was at her fingertips.

Like so many other people, Tiffany had all her social media sites easily accessible. She had the app icons on her cell's screen waiting to be tapped. Bunny grinned with total satisfaction as she hit the blue and white Facebook symbol and was directed to Tiffany's personal page. Now having a complete view of her pictures, friends list, and time line, Bunny knew trying to find the infamous Dino would be easier than she thought. In a mere matter of minutes, Bunny was blessed. In the brightest, boldest, and most flamboyant ever flyer she'd ever seen, Bunny saw her man's killer's name big as day, damn near leaping off the screen. Double tapping the picture made it increase in size much to Bunny's delight. As she studied the zoomed-in image, she saw the date of

"Dino's Prebirthday Turn Up" was that very same night. Bunny couldn't believe her eyes or luck. Not only did it have a contact number to reserve VIP booths, but it had several of Dino's pictures in the corner of the flyer. *So this ugly-faced mud-duck piece of shit having a damn party tonight at Club You Know! Ain't this about nothing. He out here running the streets getting life in like he some sort of a boss, and my baby gone. But I ain't tripping. It ain't no thang. All that bullshit gonna end real soon for his punk ass. Fucking real, real soon, I promise you that, bitch-ass motherfucker!*

CHAPTER SIXTEEN

It was nearing one o'clock in the afternoon as Simone pulled her struggle buggy up into the parking lot of the Mexican restaurant. Checking her makeup in the vehicle's rearview mirror, she was ready to go in and share a meal with her beau, Chase. Hoping the trained detective couldn't see the countless crimes she and her family members had perpetrated since seeing him last, she took a deep breath. Braced with her game face on, Simone confidently walked through the front door. Following behind the hostess, she saw her lunch date had them a table located in the far corner of the room. Seeing Chase's bright smile made her return the favor. Loving the fact that he stood up and pushed her seat in for her made Simone miss her deceased father even more. He always taught her that there were certain things a real man did to prove his true worth to a worthy woman. Chase Dugan had just done one, and she was on cloud nine.

"Hey, now," he kept cheesing, happy to see her.

"Hey, yourself, Chase. How are you?"

"I'm great now that I'm seeing you. You're looking great as usual . . . beautiful smile; gorgeous face . . . the entire package. Everything a man would want or need in his life."

Simone blushed. Automatically, she forgot the real reason she'd taken him up on his out of the blue offer to have lunch. She was here to pump him for information about the criminal cases he was trying to solve, not

behave like some immature schoolgirl with a crush on
the cute boy next door. Fighting to get back on track
and not fall victim to his compliments and endearing
gaze, Simone took a small sip from the glass of wine
she'd ordered. Seeing how he was still on duty, the police
detective wisely decided to let her drink alone and just
enjoy the food and her great company. The more she
sipped the beverage, the freer she became with touching
her lunch partner's arm, then face, then leg. Simone had
a lot of stress and guilt she'd been holding onto for the
past month, and the wine she was consuming seemed to
ease her troubled mind.

Munching on nacho chips and salsa, the jubilant
couple exchanged what had been going on in each other's
lives. Even though Simone Banks was a little tipsy, she
still managed to use her womanly wilds to unearth con-
fidential information. He had no more real solid leads in
the bank robbery case. Detective Dugan let it slip that not
only did his one lead in that crime run him directly into a
brick wall, he also revealed to Simone that the important
lead was the stripper that was killed the night before.

"Oh my God, Chase, that's too bad. Did you guys ever
catch the man that did that to her? I mean, he must've
been a real monster to do something like that. I bet a
place like that has to have cameras all over, so it will be
easy to at least get that thug soon."

"Yeah, cameras all over that don't freaking work," he
remarked feeling like he and his men couldn't catch a
break in these random crimes as of late.

"Wow." Simone secretly wanted to shout hooray and
do a quick happy dance as she sat still.

"So to answer your question, sweetie, no, Simone."
Defeated in spirit, he lowered his head, not wanting to
further acknowledge the fact he and his partner were
present inside the strip club when the murder took place.

It was bad enough having the chief ride his back about not being observant, but not his girl also. "Not yet. The bad part of it is we don't have any strong leads on that damn murder. It's like this entire city has gone nuts over the past month. I don't know if it's something in the water or what. But I mean, it's crazy. The crime rate hasn't been this bad in years. Even the national news is raking the entire department over the coals."

Listening to his Saturday afternoon speech on the state of the city, she was just content he didn't suspect her sister Bunny. Simone took another small sip of her second glass of wine and felt warm all over. The tipsier she became, just like touching on Chase, the bolder her questions also became. "Listen, honey, don't you think maybe the dancer girl was a bad person that probably was running with the wrong crowd? Maybe drug dealers or whatnot. You know those types of girls are always dealing in something shady. After all, she has lied and schemed to get the fellas to give up their money. Don't you think?" She tried planting the seed of thought in the veteran detective's mind.

"Of course, I do. But it's my job to bring justice to all the families of all victims; even the victims with questionable backgrounds or lifestyles," he explained with a serious tone and demeanor. "It's like these two deceased bodies that were discovered last night out by the James River."

"More bodies?" Simone sobered up quickly. She braced herself for what was to come next. She prayed this wasn't a crazy setup and the police were behind the walls of the restaurant waiting to jump out and arrest her. Maybe Chase had a wire on him and was just making small talk until he gave his surveillance team the signal to reveal themselves. She bravely worked up her nerve and repeated her question. "Did you say more bodies?"

"Yes, sweetie; two of them. We think one is a woman, the other a man. They were badly burned. Our forensics team has noted that both their hands were missing from their bodies. I mean, that's crazy, right? Their hands, of all things. How crazy is that?"

"Missing hands? Oh my goodness, that's terrible."

"Yeah, Simone. We think it might be some sort of wicked serial killer running around the city. I know it seems like a movie plot or something, but at this point, we just don't know."

"A serial killer? Seriously?"

"Yeah, I know, right? Very bizarre but extremely dangerous." He reached across the table holding Simone's wrists, slowly massaging them with his thumbs. "So make sure you and your sisters stay in lighted areas and travel in groups. The chief and the mayor are trying to keep this whole handless body thing under wraps until we have a suspect to parade around the news cameras."

The pair soon finished their short but informative lunch. Having Chase's word that he'd call her later, Simone and he headed toward the front door. Caught up in everything that was Chase, Simone accidentally bumped into a man and woman entering the restaurant.

"Oh, excuse me," Simone politely spoke without bothering to look up.

"Dang, you're bad!" the female rudely replied, causing Simone to give the couple her full attention.

"Oh, hell, naw! Not *you* of all people. You have a lot of nerve walking around the streets coming all out to eat like you just didn't do some old slimeball bullshit! The hospital called me."

"Listen, Simone, don't start with me!"

"Me? Are you serious, fool?"

"Yeah, girl, I don't owe you or that whack job sister of yours nothing! So stay out my face and keep your mouth shut." Walter didn't back down one bit. As his voice got louder, he seemed to be getting closer into his sister-in-law's personal space.

The once meek and mild mannered Simone Banks was no more. Her timid personality was a thing of the past. After all she'd been through, participated in, and seen over the past month, dealing with Tallhya's estranged husband was a piece of cake. "Look, Walter, I'm warning you. I ain't nothing like my sister. If you think you want it with me, you better back the fuck up and think twice. All that bossing her around and having her scared of her own shadow don't work with me. I'm telling you, I ain't the one," she ranted with small beads of perspiration forming in the tiny creases on her brow. "She put up with that foolishness, but trust, I'm not and won't. You don't want to start nothing with me."

"Oh, please, Walter, don't tell me this is another one of them go-for-bad relatives of that crazy whore you fake married to. The one whose money bought me this huge diamond ring on my finger and paid for our trip to Cancun," Walter's lunch date remarked with her hands judgmentally planted on her hips.

"Yeah, baby doll. This is another one of them psychopath dysfunctional Banks sisters," he replied, pointing his finger in Simone's face.

"Oh yeah, well, you make sure you tell that cross-dressing freak brother of yours the next time he tries to fight two women, my brothers got something for his sissy ass, and that's for real! So whenever you ready, bitch, bring it. I dare you!"

Simone had forgotten about Chase being at her side. Without reservation, she went full throttle on Walter and who she quickly had to assume was his dead baby's momma. The very one that got her ass handed to her at the funeral home. "Listen, Frick-and-fucking-dumb-ass-Frack, neither one of you two want it with any of us. If you think you felt our wrath that day, you best brace yourself. And, Walter, it's bad enough you stole all my sister's money to spend on this trash mouthpiece of shit ho you running with, but then you had the nerve to cancel my sister's medical coverage. You a weak-ass man for that stunt. You know she needed that insurance, and you did her like that after all she done did for your stupid ass."

"Well, forget her and you. The doctors done called me saying your sister up there mumbling about this and that like some lunatic; making all sorts of wild claims about things that couldn't possibly be true."

"What?" Simone twisted her face as if Walter was lying. Yet deep down inside, she knew Tallhya probably was up there in the mental facility telling them who shot King and Kennedy and confessing everything else she'd been a part of the past month or so.

"Hey, if it was up to me, I say let that banner brain broad rot in that motherfucker. I could care less—but not on my dime!"

"Yeah, you better believe that shit!" Walter's companion added her two cents.

Sensing things were seconds from getting even more out of control than they were, Chase stepped in. He had no choice before someone else called the cops. Trying his best to defuse the confusing situation in a calm manner, the police detective stepped in between Simone and her two adversaries. He felt like a ring leader in a bizarre three-ring circus. "Hold up, everyone. Please just be cool and let's try to keep our voices down."

"Man, who in the fuck is you? Don't tell me you another family member of this psycho," Walter flexed, now heading in Chase's direction. "You trying to get some of this rhythm? 'Cause if you is, I'ma gladly bless you with some. Come get it!"

Now in total police mode, Detective Chase Dugan took a few steps backward not only for his own safety, but that of Simone and Walter's shit-talking asses. Showing his badge, he wasted no more time announcing his title, warning the man to maintain his position and relax. "Okay, sir, please step back and lower your tone. You are alarming the restaurant's guests. Not to mention you are threatening an officer of the law with bodily harm. Do you *really* want to go there?"

Walter stopped dead in his tracks. He surely didn't want to be arrested but felt he and his baby momma were verbally attacked first. He complied for the most part but still continued to tell Simone just how crazy her sister Tallhya truly was. "Look, Simone, you and all y'all Banks is straight up nut jobs. Dude, if I was you, I'd watch my back dealing with one of they crazy asses! They all some animals, every last one of them. Their bloodline is tainted."

Chase just stood silent in amazement. He couldn't believe his ears concerning the wild predicament he was abruptly thrust into. If he didn't have such a strange and strong attachment to Simone, he would've arrested all three of them for disturbing the peace and any other criminal charges he could come up with.

"Shut the fuck up, Walter," Simone evilly hissed, ready to snap his neck in two pieces with her bare hands. "You gonna get enough of talking shit to me and about my family. We were the same folks that took your sorry behind in. You ate my grandmother's home cooked meals every single day and night, you ungrateful little nothing of a man! I swear if I saw your ass on fire, I wouldn't even spit on your ass!"

"Naw, Simone, you shut up! The entire neighborhood knows how ruthless y'all family can be when someone crosses y'all; especially that sneaky dead-ass Me-Ma."

"Who in the fuck you think you are? You can't talk about my grandmother like that!" Simone balled up her fist ready to strike, but Chase stepped closer to her.

"Yeah, her cranky hypocrite ass pretending like she so off into the church and the Bible, then sent her grandkid pit bulls down to the funeral home to clown. What old woman does that? That church she was so caught up in, The Faith and Hope Ministry, and that con man preacher is all a joke!" Walter was spewing all the Banks's family secrets out loud for all to hear, especially his sister-in-law's lunch date.

"Yeah, who in the entire fuck does that—sending her people to fight at a funeral home? I hope that old woman burn in triple-hot hellfire for that snake shit she pulled," Walter's girl bravely cosigned, causing Simone to lunge at her.

"Dude, fuck you, her, and y'all dead bastard-ass baby that's pushing up daises. Y'all all can kiss my pretty ass!" Having to be physically restrained by Chase, Simone finally left the restaurant kicking and screaming. As he escorted her to the parking lot, she was still heated and not done clowning. She wanted her fist to connect to Walter's and his bitch's face. "Oh my God, I hate him! I swear I hate that soulless Negro. I fucking swear!"

Chase had never seen this side of Simone. He didn't know what to make out of this out of the blue altercation she was mixed into. She had always been calm, cool, and collected every time they interacted . . . Never showing any craziness or even the hint of it. Even when the bank robbers put guns in her face and had threatened to kill her, Simone was still silent and reserved. Now here she was ejecting threats and having to be dragged out of a public building. "Are you okay now? Relax, Simone. Calm down, please."

The effects of the two glasses of wine had completely worn off. Instead of being in the mood to be loved and felt up by Chase, she was ready to violently lay hands on someone—Walter and his girl in particular. "Wow, I'm so sorry, Chase. I swear I am, but that man knows how to push my buttons. After all he'd done to my sister and our family, he had the nerve to leave Tallhya hanging in the hospital. That's some bold bullshit to do. I never wanted you to see that side of me."

"The hospital? You didn't tell me one of your sisters was sick. How is she doing? Is there anything I can do to help?" he asked, puzzled, not knowing what else to say or do.

Simone tried her best to defuse his barrage of questions. With a straight face, she let Chase know her sister was getting great medical care and would be all right, even though she knew Tallhya was crazier than a bat out of hell. Part of Simone also wanted to confide in him that she had to have some procedures done in the very near future that may prove to be extremely detrimental to her general health and existence, but she opted not to.

Although they were getting closer as the days went by, she still knew she and her siblings were criminals, and he was the law; certainly not a match made in heaven. Instead of being honest, she continued with her mockery of the truth. Further putting on an act, Simone promised to deal with Walter another way when and if she encountered him again. Knowing he had to get back to the office, Detective Dugan made sure Simone got in her car and left the restaurant premises. Watching her taillights turn the corner, he suspiciously rubbed his chin not knowing what to make out of her split personality behavior and all the wild accusations of sadistic behavior her brother-in-law had made. *What the hell was that? That was something I didn't even know she had in her*. Chase's thoughts made him second-guess his lady, but he chalked it up to not knowing the entire situation. Besides, he knew how and what people would say just to be vindictive.

Back at police headquarters, Detective Dugan got settled in his black leather chair. With a strong cup of black coffee sitting on the right side of his desk and a yellow notepad on the left, he was ready for the long haul. Knowing he'd be stuck in the semicool office until the late hours of the night, he took a few minutes to meditate in hopes of getting his mind right. He locked his fingers together after placing them behind his head. Leaning back in the chair, he proceeded to close his eyes. Lost in the darkness, his thoughts started to drift back to the happiness he felt earlier in the day when he had lunch with Simone. He got a warm feeling inside. The detective couldn't help grinning, thinking about how good it felt having her smile at him. His manhood started to jump as he relived the sensation he experienced when she caressed his knee, then upper leg. Thinking about how beautiful she was made him feel like some dumb kid; some crazy teenager in love. He missed that feeling and was giddy that Simone had unearthed those sentiments buried in him.

Unfortunately, as fast as Chase was caught up deeply in his emotions of what he felt could possibly be undeniable love, his keen investigative personality snatched him out of that fantasy and into a feeling that he could only describe as a living nightmare. His perfect princess Simone was a monster in disguise. In a mere matter of seconds, she'd transformed. His possible mate for life made visible her monsterlike tendencies for all the restaurant occupants and him to see. The stunned police detective witnessed her turn from a beauty to a beast firsthand. Simone traded in her diamond tiara for a jagged sword and had no problem doing so.

He knew there was something more to Simone's zero to a hundred drastic behavior change, even if she did despise her brother-in-law. Sure, he'd cancelled the girl's insurance, cheated on her, and had a bastard child behind her back, along with stealing her lottery winnings, so of course, Simone would be heated for her sister's terrible betrayal. That reaction was normal and was to be expected. But Simone wanted blood. She was on the verge of being deranged and homicidal. He'd been on the police force for years and recognized all kinds of sick minded individuals. He'd seen the type of rage Simone had exhibited earlier in ruthless and rotten murderers that were apprehended but coldheartedly showed no remorse. Simone's demeanor when trying to get at Walter and his girl mirrored those traits. It was as if she had no home training. Whatever the true reason was, he knew he'd have to figure that out later on his own time. Right now, Detective Chase Dugan had bigger fish to fry, and the clock was ticking.

Unlocking his fingers, he opened his weary eyes. Sitting upward, he reached for his sports teams' decorated coffee mug. After getting some of the strong brew flowing through his system, the detective in him was alert. With the cracking of his knuckles, he was about ready to connect some dots and solve some of the pending high-profile cases that had been haunting his sleep, the chief's, and the mayor's.

As he looked over the growing stack of papers and reports stuffed into the manila folders labeled after each individual crime, he shrugged his shoulders. *These cases are linked together somehow. If I just set my mind to it, I can see what I've been missing. First things first; where the heck is Tiffany's cell phone? Why isn't it listed in her personal property? I know she had it on her when she left that stage. Now, either the other dancer that discovered her body has it, along with the bracelet and earrings I noticed she was wearing before her death, or the killer does.* Finding the paper he'd jotted the distraught female's number on from the club, he hoped she'd be either honest enough or scared enough to come clean and admit she'd stolen off a dead person.

If that didn't work, Detective Dugan knew he'd have to put a trace on the line through the company provider. Regardless, he was hell-bent on locating not only that phone, but the person or persons that were so brazen to even consider perpetrating a crime that bold in a building full of people. In the meantime, he once again retrieved Tariq's cell phone and pulled up the last number dialed from his line before Tiffany's; someone listed in his extensive list of contacts as just "B."

CHAPTER SEVENTEEN

Thanks to the news reports and her sister's dim-witted boyfriend, Bunny was satisfied she was not a suspect in Tiffany's murder. Not fearing being arrested, she knew it was safe to go home to the condo. Now somewhat back in her right mind, she decided to return the multiple missed calls and voice mails from her siblings. Knowing Ginger would be the easiest to speak to, Bunny dialed that number first. "Hey, what's going on?"

"Oh, hell, naw, bitch! Don't 'hey, what's going on' me! Where the fuck you been? We been calling you and calling you; blowing your fucking phone up!"

"Dang, I been around. Can't a girl get some alone time? Damn," Bunny smartly responded like she'd done no wrong in not responding to any of their calls.

"Around like where? Girl, me and Simone been by your crib and everything. You know after you ain't call back we was gonna be worried."

"Yeah, I know but—"

"But nothing, trick. You know that slick shit you did going underground was whack as hell, especially considering what went down before you left Me-Ma's."

"Yeah, I know."

"Okay, then, fool, now like I said, where the hell you been, besides, of course, the strip club slicing a bitch's neck?"

"Say what?"

"Bunny, don't play with me," Ginger's voice went from female to male, letting his sister know this wasn't the time to play word games.

"Look, Ginger, I know y'all seen the letters, and I hope y'all understand."

"Of course, we do, but you still just can't disappear like that on us." Ginger's attitude grew sassy with each passing word. "So where you at now because we gotta talk and don't try to avoid us!"

Bunny informed Ginger where she was at. Telling him she had a game plan on deck to settle a few more scores, she told him to get in touch with Simone. "Y'all meet me over here. I got some shit to tell y'all I found out from that slut Tiffany."

"Cool, because we need to put you up on your dead mother's whereabouts amongst other things that done jumped while you was fucking AWOL!"

Bunny sat in the driveway of her condo dreading going inside an empty home. Spoe wasn't there for her to laugh or joke with or to fuss and fight with. It was just her and his calming spirit. A spirit that couldn't touch her; couldn't kiss her; couldn't wrap his arms around her or sadly give her the dick she craved.

Simone made it back home to Me-Ma's in no time flat. Still infuriated from her verbal altercation with Walter and his twisted face jump off, she slammed her car door shut. The amount of force she used caused a small bit of rust to fall from the bottom frame landing on the concrete. Seething with anger, Simone burst through the front door as if she was the police executing a search warrant for two murder suspects in a nursery school massacre. Finding Ginger in the kitchen just ending a conversation, she unloaded the partial 411 on not only what Chase told her at lunch about the cases he was working on, but the battle royal she was about to have with their sister's no-good, soon-to-be ex-husband and his dead baby's momma he's involved with.

Deciding to listen to the rest of Simone's wild escapades in the car, Ginger and she walked out the door and pulled off in Simone's clunker heading toward Bunny's. When the pair finally arrived, they found Bunny's car in the driveway. The door was already unlocked so they let themselves in. Once back inside of the condo, they discovered Bunny's overnight bag thrown on the couch. Walking upstairs, they heard the shower water running and their murderous rampage sister humming. Giving each other the serious side eye, Simone and Ginger shook their heads.

Ginger raised his finger to the side of his head, twirling it around, indicating that he believed Bunny had taken a couple of huge steps off into the deep end of insanity. First, the way she just abruptly jumped to her feet and skin carved their mother and Lenny up like two Thanksgiving turkeys. Then, she washed off their blood and just walked out of Me-Ma's—no words spoken—and disappeared for close to thirty-six hours. Finally, she plotted on, apparently tracked down, then boldly executed a stripper in a nightclub full of potential witnesses like it wasn't shit. Now here, Bunny was taking a shower, humming old love songs like she didn't have a single care in the world. As if she was easy street.

"Hey, girl, we here," Simone yelled out, hoping she wouldn't startle Bunny and become her next bloody victim.

Bunny got out of the shower, dried off, and threw on a track suit. Meeting her siblings down in the living room, she was ready to tell them every detail that had jumped off since she'd last seen them; every gory detail. Starting with the moment she decided to end their mother's useless life.

Simone, Bunny, and Ginger all took a seat at the table. Each not knowing what the other was going to say, Ginger, being a true drama queen, started the ball rolling. Simone knew of his antics and late illicit night of passion with Pastor Street, but Bunny was still in the dark. Pulling out his cell phone, Ginger proceeded to show both his sisters the candid snapshots he'd taken of the good-dick-having-preacher their grandmother admired so before her death. The more each sister scrolled, the more embarrassed they became seeing the supposed man of the cloth exposed. The video Bunny had taken of Ginger giving him the bomb head in Me-Ma's living room on the couch and the floor near the coffee table was bad enough, but these images seemed to be ten times worse. Ginger had somehow managed to get every possible angle captured. He got Cassius Street's good side, bad side, and most shocking of them all, his dark side. Simone and Bunny couldn't believe the nerve Ginger had and found it hilarious. They were amused that the pastor was dumb enough to not notice that Ginger was snapping away when he claimed to be checking his Facebook page and returning text messages. Ginger was so wild with it he even took selfies with him and the naked sleeping ordained man of the cloth.

"Yeah, you two amateurs see these." Ginger's smile grew wider and brighter each time a new salacious picture was revealed. "Well, these little Kodak moments along with me and my Bible-thumping homeboy's sex tape gonna get us back Me-Ma's house come tomorrow."

"Tomorrow, really?" Simone smirked knowing Ginger was up to no good.

"Yeah, tomorrow." Ginger cleaned underneath his fingernails and rolled his eyes up toward the ceiling.

"Let's just say tomorrow at church, right in the middle of service, a fool like me might mess around and catch the Holy Ghost . . . and everything else I could catch in that piece."

Bunny had been strangely quiet but finally chimed in, giving Ginger a high five. "See, now *that's* what I'm talking about! Hit that conniving sack of shit where it hurts. Those church members and them off the chain collection offerings is Pastor Street's bread and butter, so yeah, fuck his hustle all the way up."

"Well, since you in such a fuck-a-nigga's-hustle-up mode, Bunny," Simone eagerly chimed in, "I hope you know you threw some serious salt in me and Ginger's game the other day."

"Huh, what you mean?" Bunny's facial expression changed as she played with a broken clasp tennis bracelet on the table.

"I mean, damn, sis. I know you were deep off into your zone. I could see that. Me and Ginger both could see the bullshit. But, damn, your ass went all Freddy Krueger, Jason, and Michael in that basement."

Bunny innocently bit down on the corner of her lip. "Oh yeah, that."

"Oh yeah, is right, bitch," Ginger threw his two cents in the conversation. "You just went all Rambo with it and left blood every-damn-where."

"I'm sorry, y'all. I don't know what happened. I just was kinda in my zone. You know."

Ginger wasn't done going in. He had no intentions to let his sister, Bunny, off the hook that easily for going berserk, then dipping like she had a personal cleanup crew on call. "Well, I showl in the hell knows what happened. Your dumb ass cut Momma and that nigga up foot to 'fro, left blood everywhere, and pranced your slap-happy ass upstairs to take a hot shower, then sashayed out the front door leaving me and this crazy-in-love witch to do the cleanup."

"Hey, now. Why I gotta be a crazy-in-love witch? Remember me, heifer? I was the same one that was down in that basement shoulder to shoulder with your crazy ass scrubbing blood and wrapping bodies up," Simone leaped to her feet and announced as if she was seeking an award or politicking for political office. "Have you forgotten *I* was the one that rode with a bag of hands on they lap?"

"Oh yeah, that," Ginger laughed as if what they did to their mother and Lenny was no big deal.

Bunny was still in the dark, not knowing what to think about what Simone and Ginger were claiming jumped off. "Bag of hands? What in the hell y'all asses talking about?"

Simone was already standing and decided to fill Bunny in. After telling her the trouble they had removing Deidra and Lenny from the basement of Me-Ma's, then dropping them off at the bank of the James River, her sister was finally up to speed. Never getting a total explanation of why Bunny flipped out like she did in the first place, Simone and Ginger decided to just let it go, especially considering Spoe's deceased corpse was discarded at that very river as well. They chalked it up to the small bit of crazy that was rumored to flow through their bloodline.

"Oh yeah, so while I have y'all attention, let me tell y'all the entire way lunch went down with Chase. Like I was telling Ginger back at the house, things were all good with me and him while we were eating. I mean, real, real good." Simone had a huge smile showing all her perfectly lined teeth. "He told me they did discover Momma and Lenny's bodies."

"What?" Bunny blurted out, still on the verge of panic.

Simone put up her hand for Bunny to calm her nerves. "Naw, sis, don't worry. At this point, like the rest of the bodies they find there, rest in peace, Spoe and Tariq, they don't have any real leads; just speculation."

"Oh, whew, that's good." Bunny placed one hand over her heart and fanned her face with the other. "But what about . . ."

Simone reassured Bunny as well as Ginger that her detective boyfriend had absolutely no idea Bunny Banks was the one that sent Tiffany home the night before. That they were the ones that not only robbed the bank and set Ghostman up, but had killed two people in cold blood. When they were both over that much-needed relief of not going to prison by sunset, Simone hit them with the last part of her lunch. The part that she knew would surely cause them to become just as enraged as she was when it was going down in real time. "Okay, now both of you get ready to hear this bullshit right here."

Bunny and Ginger's full attention was on their sister. After being blessed with the knowledge that they had dodged the bullet of the law, well, at least temporarily, they couldn't imagine what else was more outrageous than that. "Tell us," they both begged, sitting on the edge of their seats.

"Well, when Chase and I were leaving, I bumped into a ratchet female by mistake."

"And . . .?" Ginger's eyes bucked, waiting for the story.

"And right off rip, I told the rat 'excuse me,' because it was on me. So you know saying my bad was nothing, you know."

"Okay and . . . Just hurry up and spill the tea, bitch. Who was she? Damn, I'ma grow old waiting for you to get to the good part."

"Real talk, I don't even know her name, but she straight had a message for you. A serious message for that wild ass!"

"For who?" Ginger sucked his teeth as if Simone was lying. "I know you ain't talking about me. Girl, bye. I don't even know who you talking about."

Simone laughed. "Yes, the hell I am; a message for you, that's who."

"What kinda message some random ho got for me?" Ginger got loud and stood up.

"Sit your ass down, Ginger. Well, umm, she said to tell your special brand he/she butt the next time you jump on two women at a funeral home, you gonna get your ass handed to you on a silver platter."

"Oh, hell, naw! Not that lightweight bitch of all bitches! Her and her girl don't want it with me, Bunny, or Tallhya timid ass no more."

Simone told Bunny and Ginger all the things the smart-talking female was blowing out of her mouth. When she had them good and heated about that, Simone hit them with the fact the skank was with Walter. "Yup, y'all. And then *boom* went the dynamite! I was on that trick's head. He started bad-mouthing all of us and Tallhya, and that raggedy good thieving buster even had the balls to drag Me-Ma's name through the mud."

"One day soon, Walter gonna get his for messing over our family," Bunny vowed, meaning every word she was saying. "As soon as I get rid of this other situation I got brewing tonight, his nickel-slick ass is next! I'm sick and tired of motherfuckers thinking they can just do or say any damn thing, and it ain't gonna be any consequences to they actions. That shit is a wrap with me. I ain't buying off into the crap anymore."

Simone immediately peeped game and fell back. She took Bunny's tone and demeanor as an indicator someone or something was gonna feel her sister's unpredictable vicious wrath really soon. "Look, sis, me and Ginger done hogged all the conversation. You did call us over here to talk. So why don't you fill us in on what really jumped off at the strip club last night—your version?"

"I will. First, let me get us a taste of a little something so we can get our minds right. I'm about to put in some more work tonight; some *overtime* in the gangsta department. And I'ma need for y'all to have my back." Bunny got up disappearing into the kitchen to grab the much-needed spirits. Seconds later, she returned with a chilled bottle and three glasses in hand. "Everybody take a few sips because what I'm about to tell y'all about to probably be the realest shit the Banks sisters ever about to do."

Simone took a deep breath as she stared into Bunny's eyes, "Realer than robbing a bank, setting up a drug dealer, and killing our own mother? Damn, sis, pour me *two* glasses!"

CHAPTER EIGHTEEN

I don't know why I let that mess go down. That entire thing was nothing more than the devil working on me. I should have never given in, Lord. I don't know how I was so weak. I know I've been fornicating with various women, some even married, in my congregation, but like I said, I'm weak. God help me. The devil has been riding my back constantly and won't give up. Please save me from his evil clutches. I'm begging for your divine mercy. That atrocity disguising itself as a woman is no more than a shepherd for Satan. He's a roadblock for your ultimate plan for me. Perched down on bended knees, Pastor Street's fingers locked tightly. In tears, his silent pleas for forgiveness for his homosexual sins his religion condemned bounced off the inside of his brain louder than any noise he'd heard before.

With the wetness of his tears soaking the front of his expensive silk shirt he didn't know what to do or what to say next. Pastor Street had not only disrespectfully violated the inner sanctuary of the church, but also the Word of God. He felt he'd smeared the name of Jesus Christ in his office. He and Ginger were both sinners, yet he could only repent for himself. *I know this thing is gonna come back to bite me in the ass—excuse my language, God—but you know my heart. I know I've been here before in this same type of situation a few years back, but this is much different. I don't know. I just don't know.*

***

"Hey, baby, I thought I'd find you here. Why didn't you answer my calls?" One of his female parishioners, the church bookkeeper, tapped him on the shoulder with her set of building keys in hand.

"Oh, hey, what are you doing here?" Cassius looked up, shocked someone was inside the locked building with him, yet alone seeing him like he was.

"Oh my God, why are you crying? What's wrong, baby?" Katrina leaned over, attempting to wipe his face but was met with him avoiding her touch.

"Nothing is wrong with me, Katrina. I'm just praying, that's all," he lied, not knowing what else to say. After all, it wasn't like he could be honest with her . . . or anyone else, for that matter. What was he gonna say; I'm asking God to remove craving the taste of a hard dick in my mouth? Hell, naw. That declaration of truth could never work. Pastor Cassius Street announcing that statement would be the scandal of the church, the city, state, and the world.

"Well, I hope you were praying for this hot and wet pussy right here." She raised her skirt, revealing that she had no panties on. Using one finger, she slowly traced the outline of her cat, hoping to arouse the man she'd been sleeping with for the past six months after she persuaded him to stop sneaking around with the elder deacon's granddaughter. Offering him her retirement fund equity for new clothes and the down payment on a summer home near the coast, she felt he was hers.

Trapped by his guilt, he looked away from her. Still wanting forgiveness for his sinful ways, he focused his sights on the hand carved cross that adorned the pulpit. Feeling like he needed strength, he whispered for God to help him be strong enough to say no to this temptation. "Umm, look, I'm not trying to be rude, but not now. I have a gang of things on my plate I'm dealing with."

"Like what?" Katrina fired back with persistence, ready to get her sexual needs satisfied. "I know whatever you're dealing with ain't better than what I got for you!"

"Please, Katrina, not now. Why don't you just go home, and I'll see you at service tomorrow? I need to be alone to think, please."

Not readily wanting to take no for an answer, she asked him if he was sure of his decision, this time exposing her lace bra with her double Ds practically spilling out of her unbuttoned blouse. Finally convincing her he wasn't interested in any sexual exploits for the evening, he walked the horny female to the door. Being a gentleman, he watched the church's loyal but promiscuous book-keeper to her car.

Going back into the church, then his office to sit down, his heart and mind were heavy. Knowing he needed to relax, the pastor reached for his Bible for comfort. Before he knew what was happening, he'd lost his religion once more. Wild flashbacks of Ginger and him doing what they did the prior night commandeered his brain. Without reservations of betraying his promise to the Lord, the preacher's right hand was tightly wrapped around his manhood as the left gripped at the tissue-thin pages of God's Word.

CHAPTER NINETEEN

Shocked at the incredible bombshell updates Bunny told them, Simone and Ginger were basically speechless. Her dramatic tales of the last thirty-six hours were that which Academy Award–winning movies were made of. Disclosing the blow-by-blow details of the moments leading up to her going into the women's bathroom at the strip club, until the very second she caused Tiffany to take her last breath, the pair sat motionless.

Simone's jaw dropped wide open while Ginger bit at the sides of her acrylic fingernails. They couldn't believe the nerve Bunny had to pull such a bold feat, knowing there were so many people around. Then have the balls to have the dead girl's bracelet and earrings on the table, saying they were "souvenirs" of the great night she'd had butchering the female. The sheer determination that festered inside Bunny's soul to avenge Spoe's untimely death was to be admired by any gangster that hustled around the entire country. She seemed to be operating on a much different mental brain wave than they were. Bunny was focused. The one-track-mind vixen was set on taking those out she felt was responsible for Spoe's death from the land of the living. As they listened to her new plans to bring Dino to task next, the plot thickened and attitudes heightened.

"That piece of slimy gutter trash thought she was just gonna walk these city streets free and clear? Walk around

here carefree like she ain't did jack shit to me and mines? I
don't freaking think so. Not on my motherfucking watch.
Trust that!" Bunny's rage could be felt with each word
that flowed off her angrily poked lips. "She be setting
niggas up and think the shit is all good." Bunny saw the
expressions on Simone and Ginger's faces and still tried
to justify her thought process. "I see how y'all looking at
me. I mean, I know Spoe wasn't no damn saint, not by a
long shot. I know he and Tariq was going around robbing
dudes and getting paid, but they wasn't killing nobody
like that nigga, Dino, did. Y'all know they was on some
take-and-go type of shit; robbery—not murder."

"Bunny, you know I love you—me and Ginger both,"
Simone stated as Ginger nodded in total agreement. "But you
do know the people Spoe and Tariq robbed probably had to
pay someone back that money or get killed. They had bills
to pay and financial obligations to their families whether they
were drug dealers or not so—"

"That is true, Bunny," Ginger spoke up, also not trying
to seem as if she was going against her blood or contra-
dict her statements. "We love Spoe and his homeboy,
Tariq, just like you, but—"

"Say *what* now?" Jumping up from the table, knocking
over her chair, Bunny was starting to get irate. She could
hardly contain herself from screaming at the top of her
lungs. "*Seriously,* y'all? For real? That's fucked up. Y'all
ain't got my back now?"

"Naw, Bunny, wait," Ginger protested, but sadly, it fell
upon deaf ears.

"Naw, girl, *you* wait. Y'all sitting here at the table in the
condo my baby paid for with that stolen money talking
against him! That's foul as hell!"

"Bunny, whoa, whoa, whoa! Slow down, love. It ain't
like that," Simone also tried relentlessly to defuse her
sister's anger, but it wasn't working. "We are just saying
that—"

"Naw, sis. That's real messed up. Now y'all starting to sound like that pole-swinging-for-dollars tramp, Tiffany . . . blaming Spoe for his own death."

"Bunny, please stop talking like that," Simone begged, not liking this side of her sister she was seeing. "You taking what we saying the wrong damn way. Calm down."

"What other way is it to take? I heard what y'all said!"

"Bunny, stop it! You bugging out for nothing!"

"Naw, y'all straight tripping; acting like he wanted to die or something. I thought y'all had my back. I can't believe y'all two funny-acting bitches right about now! Ain't this some real bullshit!"

Simone loved her sister dearly. She always did and always showed Bunny the utmost respect. The honest fact that she and Spoe lived off ill-gotten gain didn't bother Simone one bit. Although she tried her best to never need to borrow anything from her generous sister because of its origins, she never once judged. Even when she found out she needed the special medical procedures, she didn't want to turn to them. However, she did find a small bit of contempt for Bunny as of late. Even though they'd made a pact since small kids, Bunny was stretching the needle-drawn blood bond to the limits. Me-Ma was a strong supporter of their family charter; if one of the Banks was mad, they were all mad; if one fought, the other fought; and if one was hurt or in trouble, they all were. Bunny had them rob the bank to pay off her and Spoe's debt to Ghostman, which resulted in them having no choice but to eliminate their own mother, Deidra, and her sidekick, Lenny.

Now she wanted them to aid her in making sure this dread-head guy from New York received the same fate as their recently departed mother. "Look, Bunny, you going way too far with this. You need to slow down and think this plan through. We're already living on the edge of the shit we've done recently. It ain't been nothing but God that has stopped us all from being in handcuffs and facing life in prison. Why push our luck? You gotta think! Please!"

Bunny's verbal tirade aimed at her siblings continued. Unable and unwilling to endure any more of the unwarranted attack, Ginger also got in his emotions. Subscribing to the same thought process as Ginger, Simone headed toward the front door, signaling to Ginger she was ready to go. As Ginger reached for the car keys, Bunny ran over, blocking the way.

"Hey, now, I don't give a shit if y'all two weak punks wanna go against the grain. It's all the way good with me. I like rolling solo anyhow. But the other thing I need to know is when we splitting up the bread from the bank robbery? I got shit to do with my share—tonight."

Simone twirled around on her heels ready to put Bunny's hissy fit to rest. "Hey, what did we all agree upon? You wanna get us all knocked or something because you having one of your famous temper tantrums? That shit ain't right, sis, neither is this shit you trying to pull!"

Bunny stood back out of the way of the door. She was a few seconds away wanting to jump on both Simone and Ginger if she didn't get her way. With her arms now folded, daring them to leave without an answer to her question was definitely going to be a gateway to doing just that. "Temper tantrum? Is that what you think I'm doing by asking for my share of the money? Ain't that a fucking trip!"

"Look, you crazy-acting bitch," Ginger interrupted, anxious to go back to Me-Ma's and log onto his laptop. "You keep running around here tonight saying we being fake and we ain't keeping it a hundred with you. And we ain't keeping it real—"

"Yeah? Well, y'all ain't!"

"Wait, hold up, bitch. I ain't done with what I'm saying."

"Well, speed the hell up, then. I told y'all I got shit to handle tonight! I need mines!"

"Okay, girl. Now you trying to strong-arm and act a fool so you can get what you calling your share of the money. Is that right?"

Bunny sucked her teeth, knowing she needed some extra money to floss with later tonight if she hoped to pull off her plan to entrap Dino at his prebirthday party. "Yeah, so what? I need some of my share. What's the fucking big deal? I held my own just like y'all did that day. Now I want to get paid. What's due me!"

"The big fucking deal is I'm about to give you a double dose of reality in your keeping-it-real diet." Ginger's usually feminine-toned voice was three octaves deeper as she began to read Bunny. "You know good and damn well we had a plan. Now me and Simone got stuff we need to do too, but you don't see us breaking the plan or no bullshit like that. And if you wanna keep shit official, bitch, your greedy ass done spent your share when you paid Ghostman ass off. Or did you just conveniently *forget* about that huge chunk of money that went to you? Do you need me to jog your fucking memory?"

"What?" Bunny was dumbfounded. Momentarily silent, she then tried flipping the script like most people did when they are wrong and caught out there. "What are you talking about, Gene? That shit was my idea in the first place, so what? Y'all lucky I cut y'all a piece!"

Ginger immediately got more pissed at his sister and the situation in general. Here, Bunny was wrong as two left shoes and had the nerve to post up and call him by his government name, no less. "Oh, hell, naw! I know you ain't trying to diss me for keeping it real and not being fake like you said we was being. That's real fucked up, but it's all good in the hood, bitch. Do you! Matter of fact, Miss Keeping it Real, do you until the wheels fall off that motherfucker. But don't come crying to me when your ass get handled to you by that New York nigga that don't mind spilling blood, because I'ma prance my pretty ass to the other side of the room like I don't know you! For sure!"

Simone wanted to be peacemaker, however, she saw that might be a losing battle. Bunny had called them out, and that was that in Ginger's eyes. "Look, sis, how much of the money do you need? Maybe you can just spend a little bit."

"Naw, Simone, don't give in to this crybaby-acting bitch!"

"Fuck you, Ginger!"

"Naw, fuck you twice as hard, Bunny! You bugging! Simone, like I said, don't give this rat nothing. She already cashed her share out since she wanna be all technical and shit! Let's keep that shit one hundred!"

Simone stepped in between the two before they came to blows. "Come on, y'all, chill out. We supposed to be family, remember? Us against the world. Maybe we can take a little out of the stash right away."

Bunny reached her hand over placing it on the door-knob. After twisting it, she swung the door open hard, causing the brass decorative knob to knock a hole in the plastered wall. "Naw, you and this greedy whore Ginger can keep that bread. I'm tight on both y'all. Trust me, I'ma make a way to do what I gotsta do; you can believe that much. Unlike you two that sit around and wait for some random faggot nigga or your dead daddy's wife to issue me out money, I make my own!"

"Oh, so it's like that, huh?" Simone tried once more to make peace after Ginger was halfway down the driveway stepping to the car. She wanted to blurt out that she possibly had cancer and wanted to use some of the illegal funds for treatment but just decided to let it go and let Bunny bug out.

"It's just like that, Simone. I'm good. You can be gone like Ginger over there. I guess at the end of the day, all the family I truly had was Spoe and Me-Ma. And considering they both gone, I guess I'm solo out in this world. Now get the fuck on and watch a bitch work!"

Absolutely no words passed between Simone and Ginger on the ride from Bunny's condo. Both concentrating on different issues and concerns, being quiet was a welcome change from the boisterous tirade they'd just endured from their sister. After arriving back at Me-Ma's, Simone went straight up to her room to count and divide up the rest of the money they had left from the bank robbery. If Bunny was to come over and try acting a fool once more and breaking the agreement, Simone would be happy to just give her what she had coming and send her on her slap-happy way.

Ginger was already planning, plotting, and scheming from earlier in the afternoon. No sooner than the mailman had delivered several pieces of mail into the box, Ginger flipped through the various envelopes. Unexpectedly, he was met with one letter in particular that sent him damn near into a rage; a rage that could easily rival his wayward sister Bunny's contempt for seemingly the world. As if things were awkward enough between him and the good Pastor Street, now the fake man of the cloth had the real estate office sending a letter of an upcoming eviction notice and warning if they didn't vacate the property after receiving the notice, the church will be forced to get lawyers involved. From the moment Ginger had torn open the beige-colored document, he knew what had to be done.

Okay, so this down-low son of a bitch think shit gonna be all good. He think he can just send us some punk-ass letter and me and mine gonna fade off into the darkness. Yeah, right, bitch ass. Imagine that! Ginger turned on his laptop and waited for it to boot up. As he waited, he took off his tight-fitting tracksuit and decided to get comfortable. Rescuing his huge dick from being trapped backward between his legs, Ginger exhaled.

The cross-dressing male loved transforming himself each and every morning to the most beautiful female a person would want to see. The male-born diva felt he was being held hostage in the wrong body. In pursuit of being happy, Ginger, formally known as Gene, spent thousands upon thousands of dollars on medicines, vitamins, various treatments, and countless wardrobe items and cosmetics to make right what he knew God got wrong. Me-Ma had always told him that the good Lord didn't make mistakes and one day he was going to have to answer for the way he was behaving. However, Ginger let it be known to his grandmother and everyone else that chose to be all up in his personal business or had an unfavorable opinion, that God did indeed fuck up. And he would deal with the man upstairs when the time came. Standing nude in all his glory, Ginger decided to give his divine lover one more time to get the bullshit right. He picked up his cell and dialed Pastor Low-Down Dick-Loving Ass to give him his only chance to come correct.

"Yeah, hello." Ginger's call was answered in less than two rings to his surprise.

The pastor's tone was cold as he tried to keep it professional. "Yes, Ginger. How can I help you?"

"Okay, you brown-hole secret worshiper, what's the meaning of this crackpot-ass letter you had the real estate office send to our house?"

"You mean the church's house," he swiftly replied with an attitude having been interrupted from beating his meat.

Ginger had about enough. Cassius Street wanted to play hardball, then so be it. "Okay, then, fool, let me cut to the chase. Either you agree to sign back over my grandmother's house or you're going to be sorry. Your undercover ball-licking ass gonna have real problems! Remember . . . What goes on in the dark always comes to light."

"Look here, guy, I don't know what you think you have on me, but trust me when I tell you this. My people love me and believe everything I tell them. So you can claim anything you want happened, but I will just deny it."

"Oh yeah, Pastor? Is that right? Got them folks wrapped around your short little finger, don't you?"

"Yes, it is that way, Ginger, Gene, or whoever you are going by today. If you and your family want to challenge the legal and binding will your grandmother left, then by all means, do so. I'm not stopping you."

"Oh, don't worry, we will be challenging that bullshit! And don't be disrespectful, you bitch-made nigga." This was the second time today Ginger had been called by his male-born government name and didn't like that or any of the threats being made. Not one bit.

"Okay, then, Ms. Ginger Banks. No problem," he patronized the man whose dick was resting in his mouth not too long ago and who he had just been fantasizing about. "And if there's nothing else I can do to assist you today, then I will see you and your sisters in court or set out on the curb—y'all choice! One."

Ending the heated conversation-turned-argument, Ginger replayed the pastor's smart-talking voice repeatedly in his head. *This guy got it coming real soon. I can't wait until tomorrow morning. I'ma hit everybody in that church with some real amen-type bullshit! By the time I finish with him, he won't be welcome to step through the front or back doors of any church in the United States, Japan, or Russia!*

Stepping into the shower, Ginger allowed the hot water to pound down on his curvaceous body. With the wetness of steam slowly beading up on the smooth walls, he let his head tilt backward. Lost in the warm moisture in the air, his mind drifted to several of the men he'd been blessed to be with. Strangely, Pastor Street kept popping up in his sexually charged fantasies. The more Ginger fought the twisted vision of the man who was causing him and his family so much grief, the harder his manhood became. Leaning over to the metal-framed carousal hanging on the shower wall, he retrieved the bottle of fragrance body wash. Squeezing more than two quarter-size amounts into his already wet palms, Ginger went to work. His right hand clenched, and his body trembled. Up and down; fast then slow; yanking and pulling. Moaning loudly, Ginger's heart raced with anticipation of a feeling. *Oh yeah, right there. Suck my dick, Pastor Street. Suck this motherfucker until it spit up! Suck it! Suck it! Yeahhhh . . . Oh my God . . . yeah . . .* Ginger handled his business until he released all his aggression along the side of the white faux marble wall. Out of breath, he fell back from under the steady flow of hot water. Staring at the thick clumpy stream of come slide down and disappear into the drain, he felt he'd enjoyed his fantasy but was ready to put in some real work that would fuck Pastor Cassius Street up in reality. It was time for the good pastor to come clean.

Drying off, Ginger slipped on a pair of shorts. Sitting down behind his laptop, he searched through a small shoe box of black cords. Finding the proper cord, he plugged his cell phone into the computer. Looking for the settings icon on the screen, he transferred his entire photo gallery. Then Ginger proceeded to do the same to the XXX-rated video that Bunny had texted to him. Scanning through the pictures and video, he smiled with satisfaction.

Blessed with the gift to navigate his way through any and all electronics, Ginger started slicing the video, adding music mixed with still frames of the various snapshots of him and Pastor Street. Making what some would soon call a tribute sanctioned by the devil himself, the smut mastermind reminisced as each view of asses in the air, tongues on dicks, and knees getting dirty passed his eyes. *Since that fool wanna play with me, I'm gonna teach him and that entire holier-than-thou judgmental flock of his who is really who tomorrow if I don't get my way. Me-Ma made a big mistake trusting that down-low punk and not her own family. Manipulation be real as a motherfucker in life, but so is revenge!*

CHAPTER TWENTY

Bunny had taken her time getting dressed for the evening. It was her hope that the rest of her night would go better than the beginning of the day. Having had to argue with Simone and Ginger had given her a major headache and had her blood pressure on bump. She needed some of that money from the bank robbery to make sure she could floss down at the club like she needed to. She wanted to show up and show out. She wanted to make sure she was noticed. Not by just the rest of Dino's sure-to-be-on-deck henchmen, the Bloody Lions Posse, but the main man himself. Luckily, she had the diamond bracelet and earrings she taken from Tiffany to sell at the pawn shop. With more than a few hundred dollars to add with the funds she already was holding, Bunny was ready to play the role.

Carefully, she searched through what seemed like every single expensive clothing item she had hung in both walk-in closets. If this had been a regular night or a regular party at one of the elite Caucasian upscale clubs she liked to hang out at, the choice would be entirely different. However, this was not a regular night and most definitely not a regular party she was going to attend. This was, and would be, a night like none other. This night was like a date with destiny—or the devil—depending on which way one looked at it.

Club You Know was infamous with the younger crowd who liked to dance until the sun came up and get drunk off the watered-down drinks they gulped. Besides, the overpriced bottles of cheap bottom-shelf spirits and the 1980 décor, there was nothing else that stood out about that nightclub other than its known attraction of hood rats trying to come up. Bunny hated to even step foot in such a low-class establishment, but felt she had no other choice. If that's where Dino wanted to play at, then that's where the uppity Bunny needed to be as well. She had no problem swallowing her pride if it meant bringing the man who killed her beloved Spoe to his knees.

Checking herself out thoroughly in the full-length mirror, head to toe, Bunny decided to wear a pair of bright lime-color designer shorts and a cute low-cut Jimmy Choo fitted T-shirt that matched. Slipping on a pair of gladiator-wrapped coiled sandals with nine-inch metallic gold heels, she felt and looked like drug-dealer bait. With her small black crossover purse stuffed with plenty of cash, a tube of her favorite lipstick, her driver's license, and a small but sharp blade hidden in the lining, Bunny was almost ready to head out the door. Fighting the urge to at least call Simone and let her know she was going ahead with the plan even though she had to go solo, the dime-piece diva shook it off and left the condo.

Driving downtown, Bunny pulled up into one of the more expensive upscale hotels. Parking her fancy sports car in the hotel lot, she locked it up and headed toward the lobby. Once inside, she went over to the valet and boldly told him she needed a Metro Car to take her to her destination . . . Club You Know. Originally hesitant to flag for one of their frequently used cars because, first of all, Bunny wasn't a guest at the hotel, and second, the reputation of the hole-in-the-wall spot, the hardworking valet soon changed his mind when she slipped a crisp fifty-dollar bill for his trouble. Not wanting to be seen pulling up in her own vehicle with traceable plates, the car service was the perfect cover.

With phone in hand, a nervous but confident Bunny climbed in the rear leather seats of the full-sized sedan, her adrenalin rushed and her heart raced. Wanting to call Simone once more for an extra boost of encouragement, she opted not to. Before she could tuck her cell back into her purse, it rang. Not accustomed to answering anonymous phone numbers Bunny pushed reject sending the person straight to her voice mail. This was not the time to deal with prank callers, angry girlfriends, solicitors, heavy breathers, or folks who'd just misdialed. Bunny Banks had to stay focused on what she was about to do and who she was about to see. In less than twenty minutes' time, Spoe's Bonnie to his Clyde would be face-to-face with the dreadlocked monster that changed her future forever.

Detective Dugan had his notepad ready. With a pen in his hand he didn't want to mistake anything the person at the other end of the line might say. Whether their impending conversation was long or short, he felt it was best to be prepared. Praying that this could possibly be another person that could shed some light on the reason Tariq was killed and found washed up along the murky banks of the James River, he used his finger to find the recently dialed numbers. Tariq had spoken to Tiffany, and she was now dead and of no help to him and his team. The officer of the law now hoped this mysterious other person listed only as "B" would be able solve the huge mystery. Not knowing if the listed contact was male or female, the trained policeman took a sip of the strong black coffee he was nursing. Part of him wanted to just place the call from the deceased man's cell. Yet, he knew that would alert "B," who could be the murderer, that someone had Tariq's personal property, which was probably the law.

Writing down the number on the yellow legal pad, he pushed *67 before dialing from the phone on his desk. Anxiously he awaited a voice at the other end; feminine or masculine, it didn't matter to Detective Dugan long as he heard answers to his questions. Seconds later, he was met with disappointment receiving the voice mail with a standard provided greeting.

Well, I be damned; it figures. With my luck, five more bodies are liable to wash up on that damn river tonight with connections to these two damn bank robberies. Life ain't fair for a guy like me; it just ain't fair. Frustrated and exhausted, he finally decided to call it an early night. He hadn't got a good night's sleep in his own comfortable bed in what seemed like weeks. Tonight, Chase Dugan decided to say fuck the chief, the mayor, and the citizens that wanted criminals arrested and for them to pay for the multiple crimes taking place across the city. He was going home and didn't care who was against the idea.

I just wanna take a hot shower, kick my feet up on my own couch, and maybe call Simone to check up on her; see if she calmed down from this afternoon. Damn, I hated seeing her act like she did. If I could lock that no-good brother-in-law of hers up and throw away the key for hurting her, I freaking would in an instant! No questions asked.

Pouring the rest of his coffee out into the water fountain, he rinsed the mug and left it sitting on the far corner of his desk. Even though he'd left the police station and was finally en route home, the unsolved cases he was working consumed his thoughts. *Naw naw naw! Forget work and dealing with these soulless criminals that run the streets. Tonight is mine. I'm just gonna do what I said; take a good long, hot shower and call Simone.*

***

The Metro Car pulled up to the front of the club. The driver, not sure if this was indeed the location his seemingly upper-class passenger wanted to be at, glanced over his shoulder. After giving her the eye, he finally spoke, asking her if she wanted him to possibly wait until she got inside the building. He, just like she, noticed the long line of rowdy individuals posted to gain entry. Reassuring him that she'd be fine, Bunny gave him a generous tip and asked for his direct cell phone number, just in case. He happily obliged, then cautiously pulled off into traffic.

Standing directly in front of Club You Know, Bunny's expensive sandals somehow felt they were pressed against concrete that led to a surface they had no business being at. Receiving cold stares from most of the females daring her to jump in the front of the crowd and looks of hungry lust from the men, Bunny ignored them all. She knew by their crude behavior and last-chance-bargain-bin attire, they were certainly not in her league and didn't need to be acknowledged.

Not in the mood for or in the habit of taking part in the traditional waiting in line that some clubs had potential partygoers participate in, she took a deep breath, remembering the true reason why she was here. Opening her purse, Bunny took out a hundred-dollar bill. Folding it over twice, the seasoned veteran tipper made sure the one and two zeros were visible. Confidently, she approached one of the bouncers with money in hand. Wasting none of his time, Bunny quickly slipped the keeper of the peace the folded currency, making sure he saw the denomination. As he was personally ushering her inside the front doors of the jam-packed club, Bunny tapped him on the arm to see if he could further assist her in her plight. When he leaned over, she cupped her hand over his ear so he could hear over the loud reggae music that was blasting off the walls of Club You Know. Informing the six-foot-five muscle beast of a man she also wanted not just a regular booth, but an exclusive VIP booth that was advertised on the event flyer, he took her to one of the party promoters, then made his way back to his post.

"So you need one of our exclusive VIP booths, huh?" The promoter was more than happy to sell Bunny one of the two remaining booths he had available.

"Yes, of course. I need the best booth you have, please."

"No problem, sweetheart." He looked Bunny up and down, realizing she was by far the most gorgeous woman in the entire club. Not wanting to miss his opportunity to possibly get it on, he gave it a shot. "So, hey, beautiful, are you here for Dino tonight?"

Bunny played dumb just as she planned. "Dino? I'm sorry I don't believe I know who that is."

"Well, he's the one that's having the party here tonight; hence, all the reggae music, the smell of weed floating through the air, and jerk chicken on niggas' plates."

"Oh, I'm sorry. I didn't know. I'm not from around these parts. I'm just visiting, so, nope, I don't know this Dino. But if you'd be so kind to take me to my booth, I'd definitely appreciate it. I'm thirsty and want to get away from the heat that's radiating from these people dancing."

Although it was clear she didn't know Dino, the promoter knew just by her brief conversation the grey-eyed model chick was out of his range. Instead, he got her money for the booth and smiled doing so. With only seven of them in total, most partygoers either couldn't afford to be on the top tier of the club or were just content being elbow to elbow with the rest of the sweaty common folk. Whatever the case was, Bunny was escorted up the neon-lit staircase beyond the midpriced range booths, which were full of people popping bottles and enjoying a complementary Jamaican-themed buffet. Used to all the finer things in life, Bunny immediately took notice that although these people partying in this section were far from being as broke as the fools on the lower level, they definitely weren't on boss status. They were more like junior underbosses . . . which was not where she desired to be. Bunny always felt like and carried herself like a true boss, so dating another boss was her only option in life.

Feeling like a tropical fish out of water, Bunny was led to her final destination. Pausing as the velvet red rope was unhooked, she nodded at the two bouncers that stood guard on each side of the brass poles. Not more than four feet into the restricted for-true-bosses area, Bunny was met with disapproving side eyes from most of the half-naked-dressed female groupies that surrounded the tables. Smack-dab in the middle of the room was a supersized booth. Clearly, the booth with the most people hanging out, laughing, and having fun had to belong to the guest of honor. The closer Bunny got, she adjusted her eyes to be able to see through the thick cloud of weed smoke that was being blown into the air. Not trying to act as if she really cared who was who at the three-ring circus that was going on near the booth that was obviously going to be hers, she kept her head held high and her fronts up. Standing over to the side, the promoter asked her exactly who she wanted to put on her private list to gain entry to her booth. Announcing the attractive woman could have no more than seven people, including herself, he was shocked to find out she had no one to put on her list; she'd be occupying the huge space by her lonesome.

"Are you sure, sweetheart?" he asked, once more wishing he could join her private celebration. "Because if you need to add anyone at any time tonight to the list, please just let me know. I'm here for you."

Bunny looked over the promoter's shoulder into one of the many flashing lights-framed mirrors that were positioned everywhere. *Oh, hell, yeah, perfect! I can see*

*the man of the hour right over there acting like he own
the entire fucking club!* Smiling as she finally saw the
crowd move from the main party booth and head toward
the fresh food being delivered to the buffet table, Bunny
told him she was definitely sure. "I'm sorry, but I'm solo
tonight. Is that going to be a problem for me to have the
booth?"

"Look, sweetie, you paying, you staying, solo or not,"
he lowered the clipboard he was going to write the names
on and reassured Bunny that with him it's all business
when need be, so she was in good hands.

"Okay, great. Then I guess we good then. So it's just
gonna be me, myself, and I tonight. I'm having my own
private celebration, so if you don't mind, I need to get my
turn up started." Staring in the mirror at her dread-head
target, Dino, making a toast with a bottle of 1738 in hand,
she smirked, knowing very soon she was going to have
the sweetest revenge ever known to mankind. Feeling
herself, Bunny commanded the promoter to bring her the
complementary bottles of champagne she had coming
and one glass.

"No problem, sweetie. It's on its way." He excused
himself and headed toward the velvet red rope, but not
before being stopped by Dino who appeared to whisper
something in his ear.

Settling back in her private booth, Bunny checked out
the scenery, meaning the other females. It didn't take
long for her to swiftly realize she was easily the pageant
winner of the bunch. None of the half-dressed-in-cheap-
outfitted groupies Dino had surrounding him could hold
a candle to Bunny's beauty or body. *This bullshit gonna
be a lot easier than I thought. This wannabe shottas
fool, Dino, wish the fuck he could ever be on the same
level as Spoe was. But that's okay, though. Let him turn
up tonight, because his showboat days is definitely
numbered.*

CHAPTER TWENTY-ONE

Simone had taken her sweet time. She'd counted every single dollar of stolen bank money they had stashed. After doing so twice to make sure her calculations were 100 percent correct, she divided the cash up into four equal piles. Of course, she'd keep Tallhya's share for her since she was not able to deal with her own affairs. Placing Ginger's portion, and most importantly, Bunny's, in separate plastic bags, she would be ready Sunday morning to just call for another sibling get-together and put an end to all the bickering that had been taking place. Things between them were starting to spiral out of control, and that's the last thing they need if they didn't want to be caught up; division. The original plan to rob the bank where she worked stemmed from sheer necessity. Now, it was turning into an entirely different animal. The money had them all at each other's throats at one point or another since the moment it was in their possession. Simone was starting to feel as if the money was cursed after all the bad luck that'd happened; the house, Tallhya going crazy, their mother being gutted by her very own sister, and not to mention Bunny's newly found desire to get revenge on everyone involved with Spoe's death.

Knowing Ginger was holed up in his room on his computer, Simone knew from past embarrassing situations not to disturb him. Ginger was far from discreet when it came to his sex life, and walking in unannounced was definitely not the thing to do. She wanted to just toss his share on the bed and walk away, but felt maybe if he and Bunny could be back under the same roof sooner than later, they could all find peace as a family again. Going back to her own bedroom, Simone shut the door and started to focus in on her own problems . . . the fear of having to fight the death-seeking devil disguising himself in the form of cancer. *I hate this. Please, God, don't curse me with this. Please. I know I've done wrong in this world. I know I should've not did what I did to my mother, but, God, I swear I didn't know what else to do. I did it for the family to survive. If she told on us, then the family would be separated. Me-Ma wouldn't have wanted that for us. She wanted us to stay together as a unit and stand strong, no matter what. But now it seems like we're falling apart anyhow. God, please help me to be strong!* Lost in her own misery and terrified of possibly having to fight the good fight alone, the normally strong willed and strong-minded Simone started to break down. As she sobbed into her pillow, the distraught female fell asleep. In her dreams, all was good in the world, Me-Ma was still alive, and she and her two sisters and brother were still little kids seeking their mother's approval.

Me-Ma wiped her hands on her apron. She'd been in the kitchen since early morning, slaving away to prepare the perfect turkey-and-dressing meal and baking cakes and pies for dessert, along with her special homemade punch which had everyone feeling thankful to have been invited year after year. Thanksgiving was always a special time in the Banks's household. With plenty of aunts, uncles, cousins, and friends pouring in, the day was more like a huge family reunion other than a day picked to celebrate a handful of Pilgrims breaking bread with some Indians they decided to steal land from.

Moreover, for Tallhya, Simone, Bunny, and Gene, it was one of the few days of the year their wild, free-spir-

ited mother was guaranteed to show her face. Running the streets with this dude and that, Deidra Banks was well known around town for linking up with drug dealers, pimps, and hustlers of all sorts. She was often nowhere her mother and kids could find her if need be. Locating the mother of four if one of the kids hurt themselves, had a parent-teacher meeting, or just plain needed their mother's love and attention was a damn near impossible feat. Deidra cared about one thing in life, possibly two: herself and getting money. However, on this day, Thanksgiving, the poor excuse for a mother and daughter would come around. She'd always put on the perfect-parent face and con all her long-distance living relatives into donating to this and that for the four bastard kids she never provided for in the first place. No sooner than each popped out, Deidra was back searching for the next criminally minded man to be her new potential baby daddy.

"Mommy, please spend the night here with us. Please! Please! Please!" Simone tried wrapping her arms around her mother's long slender leg, attempting to get her way.

Deidra was consumed with fixing her hair just right. She'd been stuck underneath her do-good family all day and was frustrated, to say the least. Used to living life as she saw fit, she'd had just about enough of the entire wholesome environment. It wasn't her scene at all, and it was starting to take a serious toll on her disposition. Annoyed with all the chatter her children were making, Deidra stood back in the mirror. Holding the hot curling iron in her right hand and a half-smoked cigarette in the left, she aggravatingly shook her daughter off of her leg. "Damn, Tallhya, get off my leg. You're gonna make me rip a hole in my freaking stocking!"

On the verge of tears, little Simone fell back onto her right side, correcting her angry mother. "I'm not Tallhya, Mommy. I'm Simone. Tallhya is over there."

Not caring who was who of her offspring, Deidra ignored her tearful child and went on about the business of getting herself together. There was a late-night party that was jumping off at the neighborhood lounge, and come hook or crook, she was going to be in the spot. The tragic fact that she hadn't seen her kids in over five weeks at this point meant absolutely nothing. She'd collected enough money from her family members to party for days on end without a second thought of the gigantic responsibility that Me-Ma had thankfully taken over. Deidra didn't give two rotten shits about that blessed fact. She was out for self and about the business of getting high, drunk, and fucked; all in no particular order.

"Okay, look, Simone, I already done told all of y'all that I wasn't staying in this place longer than I had to. Matter of fact, y'all should be glad I even came in the first place. But hell, naw, y'all ain't happy for that much. Y'all all sitting over there in the corner, crying like some real little bitches! Especially your sissy-in-training-ass, Gene. You're the worst of them all. You gonna mess around and be straight pussy when you grow up!"

"Deidra! Shut your mouth talking like that to these babies," Me-Ma shouted, coming into the room, Bible clutched in hand. "And I've told you about cursing underneath my roof. I'm not going to tolerate that kind of talk around here or smoking in this house!"

"Whatever, lady, fuck what you talking about," Deidra mumbled, ignoring her mother like she always did. Rolling her eyes to the top of the ceiling, she kept right on curling her hair and smoking her Virginia Slim as if nothing was said. Suddenly she felt the harsh force

of Me-Ma's hand slam the Bible across her face. As the cigarette flew out of her mouth, Deidra fell against the dresser.

Me-Ma was heated. She didn't care one bit that she still had guests downstairs. Her only child was out of pocket and needed to be corrected, so she did what had to be done. "Spare the rod, you spoil the child," she huffed, ready to give Deidra some more act right if need be. "I should've laid hands on your no-good self years ago and maybe you wouldn't have turned out to be such a horrible mother to these kids! It just don't make kind of godly sense!"

"Fuck God and you too, Momma," Deidra fired back, enraged from being struck.

Simone, Bunny, Tallhya, and Gene all huddled together in the corner, not knowing what was going to happen next between their mother and grandmother. With their tears flowing in the background, the two elder Banks went head-up, trading insult after insult, followed by blow after blow. Satisfied that she'd put enough of a spiritual, mental, and physical beating on Deidra, Me-Ma ordered her out of the house. As Deidra scrambled to gather her small duffle bag full of belongings, the devout Christian faith mother demanded she only return when she was ready to be a real mother to all four of her children. Hearing the thunderous sounds of the front door slam shut, Deidra Banks's children made the pact that nothing or no one could pull them apart from each other. Of course, Me-Ma agreed. Even when Simone went to go live with her father, she still kept her word; family first above anything else.

Simone was soon awakened by Ginger giggling and knocking at her closed door. Not bothering to wait for her to tell him to come in, he pushed the door wide open. Full of excitement, he jumped on the bed with his still half-asleep sister protesting the entire time. When Simone was finally quiet, Ginger explained he probably would need her help tomorrow at church for a very important presentation for the congregation to view.

"You, Ginger, of all people, going to church without a gun at the back of your head! I must still be asleep and dreaming." Simone wiped out the corners of her eyes.

Ginger had a huge smile plastered on his face as he snapped his painted acrylic fingernails in a circle. "Girl . . . I wouldn't miss Sunday service tomorrow down at the Faith and Hope Ministry under the esteemed leadership of Pastor Cassius Street if Madonna, Cher, and RuPaul begged me to! It's going to be better than any sermon he ever said, and I believe somebody may even catch the Holy Ghost!"

CHAPTER TWENTY-TWO

Excitement filled the club. Taking in the tropical beats of reggae, Bunny bobbed her head to the music while avoiding eye contact with the rest of the people in the club. Thinking back to one of the many fabulous trips she and Spoe had taken, Jamaica in particular, Bunny almost started to have a good time posted at the spacious booth by herself. Nursing her third glass of champagne, she regained focus on the true reason she was slumming VIP style at Club You Know. *Okay, now let me get my shit back together and my mind right. Okay, Bunny, back to the plan.*

Assuming that her mark Dino had yet to notice her, Ms. Banks had to work fast to remedy that situation before he decided to leave and maybe take the party elsewhere. Sliding around the seat, Bunny seductively stretched her long legs outward. Taking another small sip from her tall flute of bubbly, she took a deep breath. It was now time for her to put her plan into full action. *All right, girl, let's get on his thirsty ass! He ain't ready!*

Standing up, she casually checked the mirrors from all angles to see who might be checking for her. Ignoring the cold stares of several females who, nine out of ten times, wished they were her, Bunny tugged down on her T-shirt, making her perfect-size breasts stand more at attention. Already knowing how her ass bounced when she walked in the shorts she had on, she was ready to make a splash. Licking her lips, she moved like a panther toward the long ice-sculpture-decorated table. Getting closer, she happily found the table was filled with every Jamaican delicacy a person could imagine. Removing one of the china plates from the stack, she was greeted by the hired servers dressed in traditional island colors. *Wow, this nigga done tried to do it big up in this low-class dump. All right then, I'll eat his little food, but only because a bitch hungry.*

Bunny had them give her a small portion of just about everything they had to offer: jerk chicken, beef patties, banana fritters, fried plantain, sausage rolls, curry goat, oxtails, stewed pepper steak, and steamed fish, to name just a few. Without reservations or embarrassment, she reached for another plate but was strangely met with some other hand grabbing the same piece of china. "Oh, excuse me."

"No problem, baby doll. You take the plate. I'll grab another one."

There he was standing there, right in her face. Dino. He had come up to her just as Bunny had hoped. Maybe not while she was ready to feed her face with some of her and Spoe's favorites, but here he was. Now she had to put her plan into overdrive. "Oh, hello, there. Naw, you take it. I probably don't need a second plate anyway."

Dino looked her up and down with admiration and visible fiery lust. "Oh no, baby girl, you perfect just the way you are. Thick in all the right places, but if you wanna get a li'l thicker in your boom boom, it would always be good with me."

Bunny wanted to be flattered, but this man that stood before her ogling her body was the same hideous piece of filth that had killed Spoe. *How dare he!* she thought to herself. She wanted to spit in his face, and then pull out the sharp blade she had concealed in her purse and stab him right in the heart. *I wish I could just kill this bastard right now. He ain't doing shit but taking up space on earth.* However, Bunny was no dummy. She knew if she really did something like that, his posse would be on her before Dino's body even hit the ground. Sure, he'd be dead, but so would she, or locked up in prison for life. Needless to say, she got ahold of herself and stayed on the path she'd planned. "Well, thank you, I guess. There's just so many great things here to choose from."

"So, baby doll, you like Jamaican cuisine, do you? Let me find out you an island girl at heart."

"Yeah, I do love most of the traditional dishes. And whoever's party this is picked out some of my all-time favorites. It all smells so damn good. I pray it taste as delicious as it looks." Bunny raised her voice to be heard over the earsplitting music.

"Oh yeah." Dino was now doubly intrigued as he semi-yelled as well. The mystery female he'd been checking out on the low since she'd arrived was not only beautiful, but loved all the homeland dishes he craved for constantly. "Well, I have it on good authority that he's a pretty all-right dude. Matter of fact, I heard these were his favorite dishes too. Maybe I can see if he can come and sit with you at your booth; maybe buy you a drink or two."

"My booth?" Bunny played innocent, letting Dino take the lead.

"Yes, girl, your booth. Should I make that happen or not? Maybe he can get his personal chef to share some of his recipes with you. Maybe come and cook for you personally."

Bunny was secretly elated. This night was going better than planned as she agreed to meet the deep-pocket sponsor who had made this entire Jamaican-themed party possible. Of course, she knew she was speaking to the man himself, but she had to play along. If Dino wanted to go through the cat-and-mouse game, then so be it. Bunny was down for anything that would get her closer to Spoe's murderer. With an extra sway in her hips, she turned and headed back to her booth. Less than five minutes later, Dino appeared at her booth with one of the waitresses carrying a bottle of imported European liquor and two glasses. He slid in next to Bunny, and she felt her skin crawl as his forearm touched hers.

"Oh, hey, you," she spoke with a fork in her hand. "I was just sitting back tasting this curry goat and vegetables. It's excellent."

Dino couldn't contain himself any longer. He had to let her know exactly who he was. His ego couldn't stand not letting the most desirable female in the spot know it was because of him that she was enjoying a meal fit for a Jamaican kingpin. "Well, I'm glad you like it. I had my chef prepare it."

"Did you say *your* chef?" She pretended to be surprised and giggled like a silly teenage girl impressed by a guy wearing a new pair of sneakers and driving his parents' car. "Wait a minute. You mean to tell me this whole thing is *you?*" *This stupid motherfucker is working on my damn last nerve; like he some sort of a real boss. I swear if this food wasn't so good I'd throw up in his face.*

"Yup, baby girl, this right here is all me. My name is Dino. This is my party, and yeah, my personal chef did all the cooking. You didn't know?"

Bunny went on with the petty charade she was playing. "I'm sorry, how rude of me. My name is Krissi. And no, I didn't know whose party it was. I'm not from this area at all. I had the driver bring me to a spot that he thought might be jumping. So I got myself a booth; well, the best they had to offer in this place, and here I am."

"Your driver? What do you mean, girl, your driver? And you paid all that money for a booth just for yourself?"

"I had the Metro Car service from the hotel downtown bring me here. And I don't care what the cost is for a good time and good service. It's priceless to make sure you have a good time," she casually remarked, knowing none of the crowd Dino was running with in the club or his Bloody Lions Posse would recognize her. Thank God even though Spoe might have run the streets to get leads on who to hit a lick on, Bunny stayed her uppity self out of the local limelight. Her face and name weren't household and Facebook-rumor ready.

"Hotel? Hey, now, girl. So where you from? Are you here on business or pleasure?"

Bunny acted as if she hadn't heard his question and started to sample more of the food on her plate. "Well, Dino, I must tell you that your choice of menu is off the chain. I haven't eaten food this tasty and authentic since I was last in Kingston."

Dino was now even more intrigued with the woman he believed to be from out of town. Running his fingers through his dreads, he leaned in closer. "Hold tight, baby doll, you've been to Kingston?"

Oh my God, why don't he stop it already? Bunny was sick and tired of him referring to her as baby doll, but she felt that must've been his thing so she went with it, although annoyed. "Of course, I've been to Kingston; several times, matter of fact. Montego Bay twice and Negril, but only once there."

Once again, Dino, the flamboyant shit-talking drug dealer, was almost speechless. In a club filled with hood rats, he'd been bless on the eve of his birthday to link up with a woman of substance and class; someone he thought was on his level. "Okay, then, baby doll, I see you. It seems like you get around."

"If you mean get around as in terms of traveling for business as well as some pleasure when I find time, then, yes, what you say is true. I do get around. Spain, Bangkok, China, Vietnam, South America, Mexico, Peru, and the Bahamas, not to mention your fair Jamaica. Yup, I definitely do." Bunny talked to him as if she was scolding some small child that had butchered the English language. *I don't know who in the fuck this ignorant porch monkey thinks he's talking to! He got me all the way messed up; like I'm one of them ghetto trash-pole-swinging whores like Tiffany he's used to dealing with. He's gonna respect my gangsta one way or another!*

It was very apparent the way he handled most of the women that he came across would not work on this one. She already was shutting him down without any effort, and he was dumbfounded. "Look, baby doll, I didn't mean any disrespect. A rude boy like me just trying to get to know you and all about you." He grabbed Bunny's hand and started rubbing the top side in a circular motion. "You think you can let that go down, baby doll?"

"Okay, then, Dino. Well, we can start by you addressing me as Krissi, my government name my parents blessed me with, okay? And not that baby doll pet name you probably call all these other women up in here that hang on your every word."

"Really?" Dino frowned with a weird smile.

"Yes, really. Do you think that's at all possible? I mean, excuse me, Dino, but I certainly hope you realize I'm not in the same category as these struggling groupies wanting a come up off their backs. I make my own money and lots of it when the opportunity is correct."

Dino was listening with a keen ear, not only the way Krissi spoke, but the roundabout way she was speaking of her travels abroad. He knew she wasn't just a chick from the hood he could treat like a piece of shit, then pass on to one of his posse members. Krissi appeared to possibly be the answer to his prayers; a new lead on a new connect or a female counterpart who was not terrified of being a drug mule. Either one, not excluding just being a fresh hot piece of pussy, he was down for the challenge. "You know what? I don't think that at all. I think you are the hottest female in here, and if you let me, I'm gonna make you mine!"

And here we go. This nigga done fell for the shit, hook, line, and sinker, just as planned. I swear I can't wait to watch this fool bleed out nice and slow for killing Spoe. Bunny sipped on the expensive liquor he'd ordered and grinned in Dino's face, making him believe that what he was saying was all good.

A few minutes of Bunny playing the role turned into a solid hour of Dino ignoring his other party guests. Posted at her private booth trying to plead his case and convince her he was indeed the man around town, Bunny had stomached just about enough. It was a hard task to even lay eyes on the dreadlocked beast who caused her world to turn upside down, but now she had to endure him trying to push up on her. When he started to describe how elaborate of a lifestyle he was living, she wanted to reach across the table and paw his ugly face with her manicured nails. Hearing Dino boast about his imported light fixtures, marble kitchen countertops, and solid gold-handle toilet he took a dump on every morning made Bunny tremble with rage, but she continued to play it off as having caught a sudden chill in the air. The icing on the cake was hearing him brag about the tree-lined wooded area that surrounded his estate. Having to contain herself from throwing up in his face again, Bunny slightly gagged knowing what Tiffany had claimed to be true only seconds before she sent her on her way . . . Spoe was chased into those woods . . . hunted down like a wild animal . . . then murdered in cold blood before being tossed into the river. All those heinous, unforgivable acts were committed at the hands of the infamous Dino who was sitting a few inches away.

It was all the normally cool, calm, and collected Bunny could do to stay in character and adhere to the treacherously intentioned game plan. Checking her watch, she informed him she had a prior engagement she couldn't be late for. Dino was visibly disappointed she was about to leave and voiced his regrets. Showing no shame, he begged her to stay a little while longer. Of course, she was not having that. From experience, Bunny knew men, or people in general, always wanted what they couldn't have. She knew she needed to make sure she was unavailable to Dino on his terms and only on hers. Taking his number while refusing to give him hers, Bunny promised to call him the next day so that they could meet for a late dinner. As she left the VIP area, she looked over into one of the many mirrors seeing Dino still sitting in her booth looking like a lovesick animal in heat.

Oh, hell, yeah! Most definitely I got his ho ass for sure! He thinks he's that deal; I'ma show that nigga how a Banks sister really gets down!

CHAPTER TWENTY-THREE

Sunday mornings were always a big deal in the Banks's household. Me-Ma would prepare a breakfast fit for a king. Everything from pancakes, bacon, ham, scrambled eggs and sausage, to biscuits, waffles, omelets, and oatmeal were liable to be on the menu. Some Sundays when she was really feeling good, she'd prepare all her breakfast treats and invite her church prayer warriors to partake before heading to a long day of two services.

Sadly, since Mildred Banks's death, her granddaughters chose to not carry on that traditional making of breakfast or church a part of their Sunday routine. However, this particular Sunday was different; at least for two out of the four of Me-Ma's grandkids. Ginger was up at the crack of dawn. Having not been able to sleep a wink, the anticipation of coming face-to-face with his Bible-toting fuck buddy was almost too much to bear. He'd taken his shower, brushed his teeth, and shaved his legs. Gorgeous dressed as a woman, Ginger was just as fine when he wore a suit and a tie and went by the name given to him at birth: Gene Jamar Banks. Only bringing Gene back out of the closet on special occasions, this was, no doubt, going to be one of those days.

After spit shining one of the only two pairs of men's shoes he owned, Ginger was beside himself with joy. Getting dressed, he looked in the floor-length mirror and nodded with confidence and satisfaction. By the time Simone had awaken and stumbled still half-asleep to the bathroom, Ginger was downstairs finishing his second bowl of cereal. "Hurry up, girl, and get ready. We need to be holding down the front pew."

"Slow down, fool! I thought your crazy ass wanted to make some sort of big flamboyant entrance," Simone yelled down from the top of the stairs. "I mean, that's what you said last night, or was I mistaken?"

Ginger pumped his brakes nagging Simone to speed up. He knew she would be ready to rock and roll when the time came at church, so that was all that mattered. Still hyped and geeked for the adventure of the day to get started, Ginger went to go stand on the front porch and get some fresh air. Deciding to smoke some weed before Sunday service, he reflected on how he hoped the morning would go and how he would be a hero in all three of his sisters' eyes for getting their family house back in their rightful hands.

The Faith and Hope Ministries choir was in rare form as the doors of the church opened. The choir welcomed in everyone with a spiritual hymn. *"Lord, keep me day by day in a pure and perfect way. I want to live; I want to live on in a building not made by hand. Lord, keep my body strong so that I can do no wrong. Lord, give me grace just to run this Christian race to a building not made by hand. I'm just a stranger here traveling through this barren land. Lord, I know there's a building somewhere, in a building not made by hand."*

Unlike most traditional message bearers of the Lord, Pastor Cassius Street was different. He was known around town for not only being flamboyant and over the top in his choice of expensive clothing he wore around town strutting like a proud peacock, but as a trendsetter in his preaching methods. He didn't wait for the congregation to come inside and get seated to get the Sunday services started; he had the choir greet them in song and celebration no sooner than they crossed the threshold.

"Good morning, little sister. Good morning, brother, and you too, Sister Mabel," Pastor Street happily greeted a family of his parishioners at the door, then another followed by many others. "It's a great day the Lord has blessed us with. The sun is shining bright, and we all awoke to see it! Praise God!" The more openhearted folk that came to worship, the more revenue the conniving preacher saw, not only in the church kitty but his pockets as well. Still somewhat disturbed by his awkward over-night conversation with Ginger—turned argument, then a battle of threats—Cassius searched the crowd of people rushing the door to praise the Lord. Thankfully, he didn't see Ginger, which was a true blessing. *Good. Maybe he and his sisters have decided to give it a rest and just let sleeping dogs lie. I wish they would just give up this silly notion of trying to get back what Mother Banks left to me and this church; well, me, anyways,* he sinisterly pondered.

Just like that, it was as if the devil himself showed up to rain on the parade of glory the preacher was caught up in. Simone Banks had just placed one foot on the stairs of the church and was heading upward. Linked arm in arm with a man wearing a suit and a tie, Pastor Street braced himself for what she possibly might say to him . . . especially if Ginger had divulged their late-night or wild-raw banging or sloppy no-holds-barred oral sex romp in the living room. Now, one of Me-Ma's granddaughters was only feet away, and he knew that could easily spell trouble. Pastor Street hoped Simone would be thinking clearly this morning and would be the normal voice of reason he'd known her to be when dealing with situations in the past.

"Good morning, Ms. Banks."

"Well, hello, there, Pastor Street. How are you this bright sunshiny morning?" Simone returned his pleasantries, still holding onto the arm of the slender-built man. "I trust all is well with you."

Stunned by Simone's nonconfrontational demeanor, the pastor was close to being speechless. Mustering up some words, he finally responded. "Umm . . . Yes, Ms. Banks, all is well this morning. I see you brought a guest to share in worship with us today."

"Whoever do you mean?" Simone looked around still clutching the man's arm.

"Yeah, who is the guest you're talking about, Pastor Street? I was born into this parish and baptized by Pastor Jasper years before you even took over this church." Ginger removed his sunglasses, then smirked. His recent secret fuck-buddy slightly stumbled backward at the sight. Luckily, there was one of the church deacons close by to catch the wide-eyed pastor's forearm.

Having his balance restored, Cassius fought hard to get the lump out of his throat that'd instantly formed, realizing Ginger was not dressed in his usual attire as a female. "Oh my God," he mumbled so that the other churchgoers would not hear him as they strolled by.

"I know, right? Oh my God," Ginger beamed with pride while fixing his multicolor print tie. Feeling smug, he then placed his shades back onto his makeup-removed face and shifted all his weight on one hip. "See, it really doesn't matter what a fly diva like me be rocking; a lace thong up my perfect ass crack or silk boxers so this caramel big-headed python I got dangling between my legs can breathe; I'm still that bitch fools love to hate!"

Simone giggled, watching the nervous Pastor Street start to sweat. "Wow, you better get out of this hot sun and get Sunday service started. I can't wait to hear what your sermon is about today. Me and my special guest, Mister Gene Banks, will be sitting front and center in the pew our grandmother paid for; the one with the Banks family brass plaque attached. I mean, that's not going to be a problem, is it, Pastor?"

Ginger stepped toward Cassius, then leaned inward. "Unless you trying to snatch that motherfucker from underneath us as well!"

With those statements from both Simone and Ginger, they rudely did not wait for a response from Me-Ma's favorite pastor before she collapsed, passing away. Cassius didn't say a word as Ginger let his shoulder deliberately bump into his. The duo then brushed by, marching through the front doors of the church, elated that they'd thrown Pastor Street off his square. Most of the folk in the building didn't recognize Ginger without his makeup and full head of expensive weave, but for the handful of parishioners that did, it automatically set their tongues wagging. Not caring that they were in the confines of the church sanctuary, they still gossiped and backbit.

By the time Simone and Ginger greeted everyone and took their rightful seats front and center, the entire church was either leaning over whispering in each other's ears or was confused about what the true meaning was of Ginger transforming back into Gene after all these years of attending service dressed however he saw fit . . . despite frowns and judgments. The boisterous tones of their supposed Christian voices floating through the packed pews were soon silenced as their always holier-than-thou head of the church walked up toward the pulpit. The choir finished singing the processional hymn and took their seats. Pastor Cassius Street cleared his throat and was ready to start Sunday services.

CHAPTER TWENTY-FOUR

Bunny woke up for the first time since Spoe's death feeling whole; like things were finally looking up. She knew her heart and emotions would always bear mental scars from the passing of the love of her life, but she could deal with that if she got satisfaction. Bunny was definitely not back at 100 percent, but she was pretty close to getting there.

Yesterday had been a true test of her patience and how dedicated she was to get what she wanted at the club, yet the beginning of the day wasn't very acceptable. Having a gigantic argument with Simone and Ginger about the stolen money and what they believed to be an unwarranted obsession with her hanging Dino out to dry had taken a serious toll on her mental well-being. As far back as Bunny could remember, she and her three siblings were thick as thieves. And even though they would have small squabbles or disagreements like most kids did with one another, they were raised by Me-Ma to never call the next person out of their name, go to bed mad, or let an outsider come in between them. Disrespectful to her deceased grandmother's memory, Bunny had broken the rules doing all three. Now as she lay in the bed with thoughts of killing Dino the next time she set eyes on him, or the very moment the opportunity presented itself, she knew she had to make things right with Simone and Ginger.

As bad as the brokenhearted diva just wanted to go underground again for a few days until things blew over with her sisters, the truth of the matter was she didn't have time, or the resources, to do so. Thanks to Spoe's greedy mother and good-for-nothing sister taking all the things of value in the condo when they found out he was dead, there was not much of a selection to choose from to maybe pawn or sell to get up on some much-needed cash. She'd already sold the bracelet and earrings she'd stolen off of Tiffany and used that cash for flossing the night before. And now she was down to her last couple of hundred-dollar bills. Bunny did want to make up with Simone and Ginger, that was true. But the fact that she needed for them to agree to come up with her share of the loot from the bank robbery was much more important.

Bunny needed that money, at least a small-size chunk of it, for later on that day and possibly the evening. She was going to call Dino and take him up on his offer for dinner and wanted to make sure she could stunt again, if need be. She'd already got the drug-dealer murderer intrigued and thinking she could maybe be a link to a new connect.

Born with a strange sixth sense, Bunny Banks was beyond excellent at reading people's true facial expressions and mannerisms. Always being told by Me-Ma that she behaved like she'd been here before and knew too much, she quickly realized all she had to do was take a little more time to talk to Dino and get in his head and he'd be practically begging her to be alone with him. Unfortunately for his thirst-trap-pussy-hound ass, it would be to his certain demise. What Spoe's loyal wifey had in store for the dreadlocked leader of the Bloody Lions Posse would be worse than any sexually transmitted death sentence disease he could catch from one of the hood rats he was used to banging raw on the regular; that gut-bucket-dead-pole-twirling-for-dollars Tiffany included.

*Well, let me get this bullshit over with and call Simone.
I need to let her and that damn crazy-ass Ginger know I
ain't got time to be messing around. I need some of that
damn money; at least a couple of racks.* After Simone's
cell rang several times, Bunny got the voice mail. Opting
to not leave a message, she held the phone in her hand,
planning to call back in five minutes. Before she could
get a chance to hit redial, a small envelope appeared
in the upper left-hand corner and a notification beep.
Tapping the envelope-shaped icon, she read the text
message sent from her sister. At church. Ginger bout 2
clown. It's gonna be a showstopper. Those brief words
were followed by several emojis that had Bunny both
laughing and worried. *Oh well, I'll catch up with them at
the house later. I know they can hold it down. I mean,
what kind of craziness can Ginger really do at church of
all places?*

It had been one of the most peaceful nights Chase
Dugan had spent since the crucial spike in crime had
started a few months ago. With what seemed like everyone and their mother on his back, he was happy to just
get some much-needed rest and relaxation. He'd turned
his cell on silent and plugged it up on the far side of the
room the moment he arrived home. Chase didn't care
how many times he saw the bright light blink in the
darkness. The exhausted officer refused to get out of his
bed. He just turned over and pulled the blanket up over
his head.

Feeling refreshed, he wanted to call Simone and invite
her to breakfast but decided to just drive over to her
house to surprise her. After getting dressed, he stopped
by the local Walmart and grabbed a small bouquet of
flowers. With the flowers resting on the passenger seat,
he then swung by a coffee shop and picked her up a large

cup of gourmet brew, hoping she liked his choice. Excited to see Simone, he turned down her street hoping he was doing the right thing by just dropping by unannounced. Parking in front of her house, he noticed Simone's car was parked in the driveway. Smiling, he got out of the car and headed up the walkway. As he stood knocking on the door, a longtime neighbor peeked out from behind her living room curtain. Giving the older woman a smile and nod, she soon opened her front door asking who he was looking for.

"Yes, hello, miss. Good morning. I'm here for Simone Banks."

"Oh, Simone, okay then." She seemed relieved and finally returned his greeting and smile. "I thought you might've been lurking around here for Ginger. You know, one of *them*."

Detective Dugan didn't know exactly what the older woman meant, but assumed whatever it was, it was no near next to being nice. "Yes, I brought her some flowers and coffee."

"Well, I'm sorry to tell you, but they went to church not too long ago. I would've went to, but my leg been bothering me." The neighbor was getting more personal than he wanted to be.

Cutting the obviously lonely woman's impromptu pity-party conversation short, the detective asked her the name of the church Simone attended just to make sure. He kinda remembered Walter, the wicked brother-in-law, throwing the name up when he and Simone were arguing. However, keeping the two estranged family members from actually coming to blows was more important at that time than focusing on the name of the church. After verifying the name and location, Chase was on his way with flowers and a now ice-cold coffee in tow. *It will be just wonderful to see her beautiful face before heading in to work. Hope she likes ice coffee.*

CHAPTER TWENTY-FIVE

Gazing out into the many faces of his congregation, Pastor Street greeted them once again as he'd done at the entrance. "Good morning, everyone. Praises be to all and welcome to the sacred house of the Lord. It's good to be here, alive and living life the way God intended for us to be." Terrified with each passing word, Pastor Street could not help from allowing his eyes to zoom in on Ginger. Trying his best to submerge his thoughts into the order of service, he kept seeing Ginger nod seemingly in agreement with every statement he was making.

As time ticked on, another song was sung by the choir, a special collection for the senior citizens was taken, and then Sister Katrina took center stage to give the revenue report, as well as the church announcements. In a tight-fitting and scantily clad attire, as always, she made sure to wink at Pastor Street, who was strangely sweating bullets in the cool, air-conditioned sanctuary. One by one, she read off items listed in the programs that were truly of no great importance to most of the bored parishioners. Just before she was about to yield the podium to the pastor to open the doors of the church for any new prospective members, Ginger stood from his seat. Standing in the front row, he smoothly turned to the rest of the congregation. With a taste for pure, uncut ignorance, he stated he had an announcement of praise and a testimony that he was burning to share. Pastor Street jumped to his feet in protest, telling Ginger that what he wanted to do was not listed in the program and highly irregular to do in the middle of the service.

"I'm sorry, Pastor Street, but if I don't say what I want to say, I might just burst. I mean, I'm so thankful for everything that you've done for me over the past few days." Ginger was acting all female as he placed his hand over the center of his chest, blushing. "I've never been so touched by a man at no time. I mean, you really have showed me that there are still good people left in this cruel world we live in."

Shaking in his shoes, Pastor Street wanted to run over and put a gag in Ginger's mouth to stop his chatter. "Please, Mr. Banks," he begged with his eyes locking with Ginger's. "Maybe we can speak about this at a much later date."

"No, Pastor. I would be less than a good Christian if I didn't share my good news with everyone here!"

Katrina, like everyone else, was anxious to know exactly what Pastor Street had done to change Ginger's life so drastically. Maybe one of his condemning-of-homosexual-behavior sermons was the reason longtime member Mildred Banks's cross-dressing grandson was now decked out in men's clothing. And if that was indeed the case, the majority of the parishioners were now wide awake, perched on the edge of the wooden mahogany-stained pews awaiting confirmation of that miracle.

"Let him speak," was one outcry from the crowd, followed by another.

"Yes, testify, Brother; speak your truth!"

Not to be outdone or not seen, Katrina finally spoke out, also asking for Ginger, who, even dressed as a woman, outshined her, to say whatever it was he had to say. "Please tell us what Pastor Street did to change your life for the good. We're all dying to know, Ginger. I'm sorry. I mean Gene," she sarcastically remarked while rolling her eyes to the top of her head.

"Okay, everyone. Well, you all know my grandmother, Mildred Banks. She was here serving the Lord in this very building before Pastor Jasper went on to glory and Pastor Street took over. She was a fixture in this church until God chose fit to call her home, right up there in the very spot our beloved pastor is standing in," Ginger pointed up toward the elevated stage.

"Please don't. Not now," he pleaded with Ginger, once more not knowing what Ginger was going to do or say next. The beads of sweat turned into a shower that couldn't stop dripping off his head. He was in utter desperation for someone to stop this madness. As wrong as it was, he was contemplating faking a heart attack to put a halt to Ginger's declaration.

Ginger grinned, taking great satisfaction in watching the otherwise smart-mouthed preacher squirm. Matter of fact, it was almost the same way he squirmed when Ginger had his tongue buried knee-deep into his Bible-toting ass. "No, no, Pastor Street. Everyone needs to know just how generous and fair-minded you can be. I mean, you blessed me and my sisters, and for that, we will be forever grateful. These fine people should know what you did and follow in your footsteps, to always conduct themselves in a godly manner as a good Christian should do."

Pastor Street's eyebrows rose. He was scared to ask what Ginger was talking about, so he motioned for some of the men from the deacon's board to calmly try to escort Ginger out the side door or into his office so that they could speak in private. "We will speak later, Mr. Banks. You have my word." Hoping the deacon board members could strong-arm him out without another word slipping from his evil mouth was a far cry from a miracle taking place.

"No no no. I need to get this out," Ginger protested. He pulled back from one of the deacon's loose grip. "My grandmother was confused in her last days. She was sick and didn't even know it. Well, during her brief but deadly illness, she signed over our family home to the Faith and Hope Ministry and Pastor Cassius Street. But last night, thank God, the good pastor graciously blessed the Banks family by agreeing to sign that property back to us free and clear. He's truly a vessel for the Lord, isn't he?"

Letting his greed take over his common sense, Pastor Street protested Ginger's claim, praying at the same time that his dirty little secret would not be exposed. "Well . . . That's not exactly true. I did offer to sell them back the property, but we haven't come to terms as of yet. Like I said before, Mr. Banks, we can discuss this later. All this gratitude is truly unnecessary."

Like watching a soap-opera plot slowly unfold, the attentive congregation needed popcorn along with a full glass of communion wine for what was going to come next out of Ginger's mouth. "Oh, I'm sorry, Pastor. I thought when I spent the night with you, the terms were discussed."

"Spent the night? What?" Katrina leaped to her feet, followed by several other women he'd slept with.

Simone hadn't muttered a single solitary word during the whole service. After texting Bunny back that Ginger was about to go ham, she kept her head down focused on her cell. Even when Ginger and Pastor Street started to go back and forth, she stayed with her fingers tapping away on the screen of the phone.

Ginger sucked his teeth and rolled his neck in flaming true diva style. Snapping his fingers, he went on to give his tainted testimony. "Yes, child. Me and him spent the night in his office doing the do." He laughed at Katrina and all the other women seemingly outraged about the announcement. "And y'all already know and can tell from the way he prances around this stage, this brother can put on one hellava show when he wants to. The sex was definitely *all* of that! *Believe* me!"

"Cassius! Say it's not true! Say something!" Katrina shouted, wanting to know if what this cross-dressing freak was saying was indeed true or not.

As the rest of the people shook their heads in stunned disbelief and were totally speechless, some of the preacher's loyal followers tried to put a muzzle on the accusations Ginger was making. Physically having to be restrained from the small but fiery protective group of prayer warriors, Ginger stood by his statements spewing even more words of his brutal truth. "I'm sorry if you all think this dude is anything more than a sheisty con man running game on all you silly-ass women. He's been playing all of you for fools. And all you men who think your wives are safe and he's just giving them a little bit of one-on-one Bible Study sessions when you're at work slaving away to make ends meet—think again. You dummies out punching the clock, and he punching your wives' cat with his manhood."

Pastor Street's pride was damaged, but he still managed to try to stand tall and deny Ginger's awful claims of his vile sins and him breaking every one of the Ten Commandments. "You are nothing more than an abomination against mankind and Almighty God. You think you can come into this sacred sanctuary and defile my name? You are nothing more than a liar and a bearer of false witness. You already have signed a pact with the underworld and sold yourself to the devil! You are nothing more than a freak of nature; an extremely confused, worthless human being. Walking around town, and worse than that, coming through the doors of this church violating his Holy Word!" Pastor Street was sweating up a storm. Putting on a performance of a lifetime, he condemned Ginger, Simone, Bunny, Tallhya, and even the church's beloved lifetime supporter, deceased Mother Mildred Banks, for condoning Ginger/Gene's wicked ways and disgusting lifestyle. "People like you should be thrown in an open dirt pit and burned alive! Amen! Get this abomination out of our church!"

Ginger's skin was extra thick. He'd learned a long time ago to let other people's opinions of him and his lifestyle choice roll off his back. Labeled "different" since birth, Ginger had been picked on as a small child growing up on the block. And maliciously ridiculed by his own mother for behaving too girlie. Called a sissy in grammar school and a fag in junior high, by the time the bullied youth reached puberty and had become a teenager, wearing lip gloss and his sisters' panties were second nature to him. Going against the grain, Gene officially became Ginger at his senior prom when he showed up proudly decked out in an above-the-knee powder-blue lace-and-satin skintight dress with a long chiffon train. Arm in arm with his date, Charles, he had no shame then or now. He felt whoever had a problem with him just had a problem. He wasn't going to change who he was for anyone . . . even for the sake of God.

"Look, Cassius," Ginger said his name like he meant it, "like I told you the other morning when we woke up, don't let this butter-smooth skin and pretty face fool you. I will wear your self-hating ass out! I told you about coming for me."

Pastor Street was not giving up without a fight. He'd built too much of a money-getting venture up to just walk away with his tail tucked between his legs. "Okay, Ginger or Gene or whatever you want to call yourself. You need to stop all these false, slanderous things you're saying before I decide to lose my religion and press charges. You are nothing but the devil right out in the open!"

Ginger had just about enough of being accused of being a liar and the devil, being a fag and an abomination from a first-class hypocrite. It was time for this so-called man of God that specialized in bringing judgment against others to be judged. "Nigga that hides behind the damn Bible and God's so-called Word, you up there talking that yang yang shit about me—like you better than me!" Ginger's voice got louder as all the congregation looked on in shock at what was taking place at their normally uneventful Sunday service. "Well, guess what, you fraudulent asshole? You *ain't* better than me! The truth of the matter is, you *is* me! So hello, my devil brother!"

Ginger had gotten his way and for once he was the hero of the Banks and not just the family freak.

With that being said, complete and total pandemonium ensued throughout the church dwelling. Simone had started sending group text messages to each and every person's phone number listed in the church directory. Thanks to Me-Ma also having the numbers of all the highly revered prayer warriors as well, the entire church was on their feet. Young and old, they couldn't believe what they were watching. It was like some sort of bad dream. Pushing play repeatedly, the women of the church Pastor Street had sexed held their cell phones, worried what disease this biblical monster could've subjected them to, while the men were ready to throw the twisted-thought preacher out on his head. There was nothing the preacher could say or do.

The pornographic smut had been sent to the good pastor's cell as well. Not only were there clips of him and Ginger partaking in oral sex in Me-Ma's living room, but selfies of them hugged up in the church office while he was asleep and audio of his voice saying basically that he takes advantage of women's kindness when need be. The loyal members of the Faith and Hope Ministry were enraged.

This was the type of scandal that could bring the church down to its very foundation and have its doors chained, locked, and bolted for good.

Pastor Street didn't know what to say. Here he was standing in front of everyone with all his dirty laundry aired out for all to see. He'd been exposed for the greedy predatory creep he was. Destined to be shunned, he lowered his head, disappearing into his private office before he was literally killed. Shame and embarrassment held him locked in his office until the board of trustees came banging on the door. He paced the floor, trying to come up with a plan to turn everything around. *Everything was photoshopped . . . That wasn't me. I can deny the women of the church I slept with. They wouldn't want their husbands to think they've done wrong.*

"Pastor Street, you must open this door immediately. There are matters we must discuss at once."

With his hands shaking, the pastor unlocked the door. Before he could spin his lies, he was halted by one of the board members.

"Pastor Street, this is outrageous! I thought you were a man of God! That video has been seen by the entire congregation. What do you think our church affiliates will think?"

"That video was the true devil in disguise. That is not me! The devil must've pasted my face to make it look like me. You can't believe that abomination is showing you the real truth." He hoped for a listening ear that could help his fight.

"I can't believe this!" another board member shouted.

"Brothers, you can't truly think I would be shaming the house of God and disrespecting the Word of God in this most outrageous way. Brothers, Sisters, you can't believe this. I'm not that person in those pictures or that video."

"I'm sorry, Pastor, but this kind of scandal can close the church's doors. We must do what's necessary. Please clear your office of your personal items and vacate the premises immediately."

"But . . . But you're not even giving me a chance to speak my truth. I am a man of God and will never bow down to this type of malicious accusations without the right to disclose my truth. This is shameful. What you all are doing to me is unlawful against the church! I can't—and won't—stand for this!"

"Okay, then, let's take a proper vote." The head board member looked around and proceeded. "All those in favor of Pastor Cassius Street to be formally stripped of his robes and connection to Faith and Hope Ministry permanently, please raise your hands."

Former Pastor Cassius Street looked around the room seeing a unanimous vote for his immediate removal, then bowed his head in shame. Forced by the board of trustees and the prayer warriors to immediately sign over the deed to the late Mildred Banks's home and all other dealings attached to her estate, Cassius Street was ultimately disgraced and immediately discredited by the church and all their affiliates from surrounding churches in the area.

"Brothers and Sisters, I believe we have a lot of work ahead of us, and in light of today's events, I think it's best we go home, collect our thoughts, and pray on our impending dilemma. We should meet back here at seven tonight to discuss the future of our beloved church."

All heads nodded yes and quickly dispersed to calm themselves after the storm swooped in earlier, leaving the entire congregation in an uproar. When the board members left the church, they were bombarded with questions by the awaiting members of the church.

"Brothers and Sisters, please, please . . ."

"I want all my donations back! This ain't no church. It's the pit of hell with all this going on," a member shouted.

"Now I understand everyone's concern, and we will address it, but we can say the former Pastor Street is no longer a part of this church or will be of any other after I get through talking to everyone. Now, it's been a trying morning, and well, to tell you the truth, I think we all need to go home and process what has taken place."

There was disappointment heard throughout the crowd gathered, but there was nothing more to be done to correct the damage already displayed.

Although his elusive career was no more, there was more trouble brewing for the former renowned-now-defrocked-and-disgraced pastor. As he snuck his way out of the back of the church and quickly jumped into his car, his phone blared off with text alerts, calls, and even e-mail notifications. He tossed it onto the passenger's seat and pulled off toward his home. The only thought on his mind was how he could recover from this cruel and malicious incident that cost him everything. Tears began to flow, combined with shouts of anger. "You are so stupid! Why didn't you just give them the stupid worthless house? You could have gotten way more in the long run!" He banged on the steering wheel, mad at himself about his greedy actions.

He pulled into his driveway and noticed a familiar car already parked. Cassius's first reaction was to make a U-turn and get the hell outta Dodge as fast as fucking possible. But when he saw the woman strutting toward his car, he knew he would have to eventually face her, and many others that were indulging in his "special" Bible lessons. This was just the first of many.

"Cassius Street, get out of that fucking car now!" Katrina waved her hands as if she was directing a child.

With much hesitation, he slowly parked beside her car, turned the ignition off, and stepped out of the vehicle.

"What in the fuck is you doing? Did you fuck that freak?"

Still in the driveway, Cassius decided on taking this indoors. He sure as hell didn't want the neighbors in his business, and by the tone of Katrina's voice, they soon would come out to see the show. "Let's go inside before you embarrass yourself." He touched her arm to guide her toward the door.

"Fuck you! I ain't going nowhere with your lying ass, you fucking faggot!"

"Please, this is ridiculous that you are even acting this way. Let's go inside, please, Katrina. I can explain everything."

"No, because I have already warned the board that you swindled me out of my retirement money, and they have agreed to pay for all the lawyer fees to press charges on you."

"Oh, is that so!"

"Yes, and by the way, I am pregnant, you stupid piece of shit!"

"What makes you think it's mine? If you fucked me behind your husband's back, who's to say you ain't spreading your legs for another? Now you can leave, or I can call the cops to remove you from my property."

"You piece of fucking shit! As much as I dislike the Banks, I'm going to send them some flowers for the shit show they put on today for outing you."

Cassius watched Katrina stomp to her car still enraged, but he could care less. It came with the territory. Some just play the game better than others. He unlocked his front door and walked inside, struggling with thoughts of what his next move should be. *It's time to blow this joint!*

CHAPTER TWENTY-SIX

Simone and Ginger left through the church doors the same way they had entered . . . arm in arm with smiles on their faces. They felt they were victorious, and it showed in their steps as Ginger held the deed to their grandmother's house in hand. Still hearing the loud panicked voices of folks trying to figure out what had just jumped off and the possible ramifications, the pair was smug. Knowing that their long lineage of family loyalty to that church had come to an abrupt end as of today meant absolutely nothing. Truth be told, when they'd put Me-Ma in the grave burying her, their allure to the church was buried as well. Three feet away from the church stairs Simone was stopped dead in her tracks. She couldn't believe her eyes. She was surprised, to say the least. Chase Dugan, of all people, was leaning against his car. Not knowing what he could've wanted, Simone hesitantly made her way over to his car as Ginger went to his own.

"Well, hello?" she suspiciously spoke with question.

"Hello, yourself, Simone." He raised his eyebrow and smiled.

Relieved he wasn't there to arrest her and Ginger for multiple crimes they'd committed, including murdering their mother, Simone loosened up some and returned his smile. "What are you doing here? Matter of fact, how did you even know I was here? Are you using your police tactics to follow me now?"

"Umm, no, not at all. Your nosy neighbor next door told me," he laughed. "We need her on the damn police force. She sees everything and will let you know, even if you didn't want to know!"

Simone agreed, having grown up next door to her grandmother's porch gossip buddy. "Well, wow, Chase, I am glad to see you. We kinda got out of church earlier than everyone else."

Chase could not contain himself any longer. He had to let her know he'd slipped in church at the end of the first collection for the senior citizens, right before the girl with her boobs hanging out started to read the announcements. "Yeah, Simone, about that . . . I ain't gonna lie. I normally don't go to church; I don't really have the time. But after today, and how your brother blew the spot up . . . It was priceless. I swear on my badge I've never seen or heard anything like it. It was like watching some bad movie that comes on late at night."

Simone's facial expression was that of being confused. She was embarrassed that a guy that she was dating and actually liked saw and heard her family secrets get revealed live and in person. It was bad enough the family was going to probably be shunned from even speaking to most folks Pastor Streets's charities helped, but now she had to contend with this. "Look, Chase, I don't know what to tell you. That slimeball preacher stole, well, manipulated, my grandmother's house away from her shortly before she died. We just wanted it back, that's all."

"Yeah, I see. You and your family play hardball just like your brother-in-law said. Remind me not to get on your bad side!"

The mere mention of Tallhya's husband's name pissed Simone off, making her blood boil. "Yuk, please don't say his name. You know we can't stand him."

Chase agreed not to hint at Walter's name again as he reached in the rear seat of his vehicle, handing Simone the flowers he purchased. "I had some coffee too, but of course, it's no good unless you like cold coffee."

Deciding to ride with Detective Dugan back to Me-Ma's, Simone called Ginger telling him she was good on the ride tip, and she'd see him at home. At that point, he informed her he was going to hang out with a few of his friends in the LGBT community and celebrate his victory over the fake down-low, hate-spewing Pastor Street.

Pulling up in front of the house, Chase quickly observed an expensive sports car parked in the driveway behind Simone's Neon that wasn't there earlier. "Wow, that's a really nice whip. I know that hit someone's pockets hard."

Not wanting him to get the wrong impression and think she and her siblings had money or access to it, Simone played it off. "Oh, that's my sister's boyfriend's car. He's some white guy that plays basketball overseas that's so in love with her, it's crazy. He let her drive his car until the lease runs out next month. So . . ." Having explained her way outta Bunny's dead boyfriend that robbed the stickup man and sponsored the car, Simone was good.

Going inside, Simone offered Chase something to drink and told him to take a seat in the living room. Walking upstairs she found Bunny in Ginger's bedroom plugging in the flat irons. She knew Bunny had been through the wringer and was still suffering from the loss of Spoe, but prayed shit between them could be repaired without further disagreements or fights. "Hey, sis, are you okay? Are *we* okay?"

Bunny knew Simone was making reference to the big disagreement that had taken place over at her condo the night before. Knowing she was wrong as two left feet and had blown the entire thing out of proportion instead of just taking the time out to explain her dire need for a small bit of the ill-gotten gain, Bunny wasted no time taking a cop to her bullshit. "Of course, we are. I mean, we family; sisters. What else can we be but good? That's why I'm in here using this crazy ho's flat irons. She got the best hair-grooming shit in the city, not to mention clothes I may need to borrow if I wanna go hang out in some club with hood rats! Shiddd, a bitch never know which way the wind gonna blow."

Simone was relieved the matter was finally over. She did inform Bunny she'd counted and split the cash up, and her share was wrapped in a bag in the back of the closet in her old bedroom. From this point on, it'd be on each individual to govern their own selves when it came to spending the money. Bunny was overjoyed because this way, she didn't have to further involve her siblings with her plans of Dino's demise.

"Well, Chase, is downstairs if you wanna say hello. He met me at church and brought me some flowers," Simone mentioned, throwing her hand up.

Bunny laughed as she spoke under her breath, "Come on now, dummy. Get your motherfucking life! Why in the hell do I wanna see, say hello, or even give two hot-fire shits about some slow-minded cop that's trying to lock our pretty asses up? If you wanna sleep, bang, or lay up with the enemy, then that's on you. So, girl, bye, miss me on all that! Now, beat it. I need to finish my hair. I got somewhere to be tonight."

Simone could only shake her head and laugh as well. "Okay, then, cool, but when he leave, I gotta put you up on what Ginger did today. Bottom line, Me-Ma's house is back to being ours, point-blank." With that being said, Simone returned downstairs to discover her detective boyfriend looking at the many family pictures her grand-mother had showcased on the mantle, sitting on the end tables, framed and hanging on the walls. It was like a small-size shrine to Deidra, Tallhya, Bunny, Ginger, even when he was Gene, and, of course, Simone. "Sorry about that. My sister is upstairs acting silly as normal."

Holding his cell in his hand, Chase informed Simone although he'd love to sit and visit with her, he'd received an urgent call from the chief asking him to come into the office. "Maybe we can eat a late dinner if you're not too busy this evening. How does that sound?"

Cheesing from ear to ear, she quickly agreed. "Yes, it definitely sounds like a plan to me. I'll be home all day, so just call me when you get ready." After walking Chase to his car, Simone returned inside the house and found Bunny looking out the window as the officer of the law drove off. "What you got to say?"

"Nothing to your sprung ass," Bunny teased her sister. "So just tell me what that nut case Ginger did at church before I leave. Knowing him, I know it was straight over the top."

CHAPTER TWENTY-SEVEN

It was nearing five in the evening and Detective Chase Dugan was back in the office attempting still to bring some closure to a few of his more higher-profile cases. Adhering to the wishes of the chief, he'd been working relentlessly since the very second he'd walked in. Finding out one of the news channels in town was going to do a special segment on the spike in criminal activity in the summer months, the officer's superiors wanted him to be able to give them a little bit more information than what they originally had when the day the crimes were discovered. It was told to him that the murder of Tiffany Ross, along with the more recent floating corpses discovered, would be showcased. That being said, Chase Dugan had to deliver some good news or risk a possible reassignment—fingerprint detail.

Racking his brain for anything that could save his ass, he reached in his desk drawer retrieving Tariq's cell phone. Powering it back on, the detective was once again on the deceased young man's Facebook profile looking at the many RIP posts on his page. Scrolling through them and not seeing anything out of the ordinary, he went back to his photos. Halfway through the second album, he stopped. *Wait one damn minute. Why does this picture look so familiar to me? Am I tripping out because I'm so tired or what? It couldn't be . . . or could it?* Struggling with the same photo he thought might have been someone he'd met before, Chase zoomed in on the face. *Shit! Naw. I must be bugging!* He saved the picture to the device, then cropped out the female standing in the middle with just the initials "B" listed as her name. *Son of a bitch! All this time I've been running in circles chasing my tail like some deranged dog in heat, and here this girl was only a phone call away for real.* Recognizing Simone's sister, Bunny, who was in most of the pictures at their grandmother's house earlier as the same girl Tariq apparently had known was almost mind-blowing. *Okay then, B as in Bunny; Bunny Banks. Now if I can figure out exactly why my victim was calling her before his murder, I'll be one step closer to finding out the who's, what's, and why's to this case.*

Taking his time, he went through picture after picture in album after album, saving any and all photos that had the woman of his dream that he was dating, Simone's sister, in them. *Now what does Bunny Banks have to do with this dude, Tariq, and who is the other guy in the picture she hugged up with? I thought Simone told me her boyfriend was some white guy that plays ball overseas somewhere; that's whose expensive sports car that was in the damn driveway. And what in the hell does Simone's sister have to do with the dead dancer and Ghostman, a drug-dealer kingpin that robbed the bank? Some shit ain't right, and I'm about to find out the real deal on all this twisted mess. This might be the very break I been looking for!*

Bunny called Dino and, as she already expected, he was ready to drop everything he had planned prior to link up with her. She'd fucked his mind so royally the night before, he was practically begging to not only spend time with her, but some money on her as well. Of course, the Jamaican-born idiot was behaving like any other man that had come in contact with a beautiful, classy, refined woman . . . He wanted the pussy. However, he also felt she was a direct plug to the main plug.

Dino had money to burn, and he made sure everyone in town knew it. Yet, the girl, Krissi, was much different than the other trout-mouthed bitches he usually rocked with. She acted like she had so much game, he had to elevate his own to even come close to match hers. She'd traveled all over the world. She'd seen places and eaten cuisine and had experiences that Dino knew was beyond his reach; money or not. The midlevel drug dealer knew some things were out of his reach and jurisdiction, no matter how hood rich you were. Certain people only did business with certain people. He prayed Krissi was one of those people that could introduce him to that underworld and back him on his credibility and gangster, if need be. He was prepared to definitely make it worth her while.

"So you're going to meet me at the hotel for sure, Dino? I have limited time left in town and don't have time to be held up."

"Listen, baby doll, I'm sorry. I mean Krissi. I'd never waste your time. Like I told you last night, I'm really digging you. I wanna just spend some time with you outside that noise box we were in." Dino was not used to bowing down to any female's demands, but she was not just any female, so he took a cop. "Hey, now, I know that spot last night was not top-notch, what you used to and all, but trust, I gotcha next time you're in town."

Bunny held the hotel house phone to her ear and grinned. "Okay, Dino. I believe in you, and I wanna see you as well, away from that environment. So here's the plan. Go to the hotel and grab a suite for us to chill in. I'll call you at about seven on your cell from the lobby, and you can tell me the room number. Is that cool with you?"

Dino was ecstatic. He was going to not only spend time with his opportunity in high heels; he was going to get some of that perfectly shaped ass as well. "Don't worry. I'll be on time and waiting. Is champagne good for you?"

Bunny dug underneath her fingernails scheming as she ended their conversation leaving him to wonder, "Why don't you surprise me? I'll call you at seven." Having already checked into the same hotel she'd used the Metro Car service at the evening before, she kicked up her feet and relaxed, staring out the huge picture window at the downtown skylights. In less than two hours, she'd be back in the face of Spoe's killer, and if all went well, Dino wouldn't make it to see daybreak. At least that was the plan.

Police headquarters had been invaded by the news crew cameras ready to shoot footage of the areas in the building that were equip to run different tests on crime-scene evidence. The Forensics Department had received a huge federal grant, and now it was time for them to show and tell. As the reporters filmed one aspect of the crime-fighting efforts segment, Detective Chase Dugan got groomed and prepped for his interview by the chief and the mayor as well. He was told what to say and what not to say. Although he was trained for years on how to deal with nosy reporters, they felt the need to reschool him on the art of avoiding certain questions and making the police force, in general, come off smelling like roses.

After the reporters were finally done grilling him, Chase ducked into the bathroom to wash off the small amounts of commercial powder and makeup their makeup people forced him to wear so as not to appear too shiny faced on the camera. Splashing a few handfuls of cold water on his face, he allowed it to drip down back into the sink.

Grabbing a few brown, rough-textured paper towels out of the wall-mounted dispensary, he stared into the mirror. As he double-checked, making sure no signs of the added beauty products were still visible, the wheels in his mind started turning again.

Sitting behind his desk, he used a pencil with an eraser and drew himself a graph. Drawing line after line, he detailed possible ways all the people and potential leads he'd come up with were linked. Still haunted by possible connections Simone's sister, Bunny, had to all of this, he decided to cut straight to the chase and ask Simone. They were supposed to meet for dinner later on, so it would be the perfect opportunity for him to make the needed inquiries without seeming as if he was suspicious of Bunny.

CHAPTER TWENTY-EIGHT

It was nearing seven o'clock, and Bunny was more than ready to start her date with destiny. Running hot water in the sink, she took one of the winter-white fluffy washcloths and submerged it in the water. After lathering up the soap, she washed her kitty cat, making sure it was fresh and clean. Moving the rag in small circular motions, she imagined it was Spoe's hand touching her the way he used to before his death. A few minutes into her mind being taken over by her fantasy, she was snatched out of the sexually charged trance by her cell ringing. She'd set the alarm to ring at exactly six fifty-five. *Okay, let me get dressed and make this call to this stupid-ass fool.*

Throwing on something supersexy and expensive she'd packed in her overnight bag, Bunny stood in the mirror jocking herself. *Oh yeah, it's going down tonight. That nigga Dino about to pay for it, Spoe. Don't worry, my baby, I got you!*

Walking over to the desk, she lifted the phone's receiver and pushed the number nine to get an outside line. Dialing Dino's cell phone, the eager, soon-to-be victim answered Bunny's call on the first ring. "Hello, Dino."

His voice sounded like that of a kid about to go on a shopping spree at a toy store. "Hey, now, Krissi. How are you? Did you have a good day? We still on for this evening or what?"

Bunny smiled that she had him going, but at the same time, was slightly annoyed that he came off as so desperate. "Wow, yeah. Slow down with the bombardment of all those questions. One thing you'll learn about me is that if I say I'm going to do something, then you can consider it as good as done."

"Oh yeah." Dino felt as if he was about to hook up with his soul mate.

"Yeah, dude. I said I'd call at seven, and it's seven. When I'm with you I'm all the way with you. So with that being said, please tell me you got the suite for us to chill in already, 'cause I'm really not in the mood to wait around."

Dino was ecstatic to tell her that not only did he get a suite, he got the best one the hotel claimed to offer. "Yes, baby doll, I mean Krissi. Me and you is good to go. I was going to see if you wanted me to have my personal chef prepare us some late dinner, but I don't have a number to reach you at."

"Oh yeah, that's right, you don't have my number. Well, I'm quite sure after tonight you'll have my number and a little more than what you was probably bargaining for. Is that okay with you?" Bunny poured the charm on extra thick as she seductively spoke into the phone while tucking two blades in the side compartment of her purse.

Dino hurried up revealing the room number to his dream date and was glad to hear Bunny would be up in ten minutes or so. He checked to make sure the champagne he'd ordered was chilling and the room looked presentable. He'd been watching television and chilling since checking in at five o'clock. Shortly after making sure all his traps were set, he heard two short taps on the door. *Damn . . . Okay, she's here. Shits about to be on and popping. Even if I don't get the hookup on some shit, I'm about to get some of the best-looking pussy I done seen in months!* Rushing over, Dino yanked the handle downward, swinging the door wide open. "Hello, my queen. Please, come on inside."

Listen to this damn fool-ass nigga. He gone! This nigga act like he ain't get some good pussy in who knows how long. Pitiful. Just fucking pitiful. This bullshit gonna be way easier than I thought. "Why, thank you." Bunny stepped into the spacious multiroom suite and smiled. "Wow, okay, I see you up in here doing it big; champagne chilling and even some chocolate-covered strawberries." She picked up the bottle, turning it so she could read the label. "And I see you even got us the good stuff tonight. I'm definitely impressed."

Dino was feeling himself that he'd made Krissi smile, and she was more than satisfied. After opening the bottle and pouring them two glasses, the pair sat down on the plush couch. Reaching for the huge remote off the coffee table that controlled everything from the climate of the room, the lighting, and the curtains, to the four gigantic flat screens mounted throughout the room, along with the surround sound system, he felt like he was a boss amongst bosses. His house was indeed a showplace, and he could, and would, be proud to bring any female to see where he laid his head at, but it was apparent Krissi was different, and it'd take more than some solid gold fixtures and a marble countertop to impress her. This suite was only the tip of the iceberg for what he had in mind for her. She had potential to be wifey material; the legal-white-dress-standing-at-the-altar type. He knew he'd just met Krissi and didn't even know her last name, but he believed the gods may have sent her to him to make up for all the bad luck he'd been having lately. She was like a gift; a blessing.

After scanning over the hotel menu, they ordered room service. Indecisive over what to get, Dino bossed up getting almost one of everything that they had to offer. Cleverly not to be seen by any of the hotel staff, Bunny conveniently excused herself to the bathroom to freshen up when the small buffet carts arrived with their appe-

tizers, main courses, and desserts. Finally kicking off
her shoes, which Dino automatically recognized as being
expensive, they sat down, eating, drinking, and enjoying
music for hours on end. Bunny wanted her target to be
good and relaxed so when the time came for her to send
him home to the devil, he wouldn't be expecting it or
able to put up much of a fight. The less struggle or opposition to certain death, the better she always believed.

Checking her cell, Bunny noticed it was almost ten
o'clock. Having made watching the news a priority due to
the recent crimes she'd been unfortunately involved in,
and not caught, Bunny had Dino turn the music off and
the television on. Glad to have a female that was more
interested in current events than who was having a half-
off sale on weave was refreshing to him. Together, they
listened and watched attentively, as he was just as guilty
of heinous crimes as she was and had yet to be brought
to justice for them. Five minutes into the broadcast, a
special segment was about to air pertaining to crime in
Richmond.

*"In between all the murders and other crimes, our
fair city is turning into a cesspool for criminals to feel
as if they can run amuck. Well, the chief, along with
the mayor, has revealed to our reporters a plan to not
only clean up our city, but other locales within close
proximity to ours. We spoke to Detective Chase Dugan
earlier, and here's what he had to say about some of the
more recent high-profile crimes."*

*"Yes, we are definitely closing in on more suspects
in not only the bank robberies and the cold-blooded
murder of exotic dancer Tiffany Ross, but also in the
cases of the bodies that have been discovered floating
in the James River. We will be bringing certain people
to justice by week's end. Some extremely valuable leads
have just surfaced, and trust me when I tell you, it's only*

going to be a matter of time before these animals are apprehended, charged, and locked up behind bars."

Both feeling as if Detective Dugan was speaking to them, their demeanors somewhat changed. Bunny was the first to speak out on the segment. "Wow, so it looks like this city is about to get hotter than July; you think?"

"Maybe, maybe not. I mean, there's always crime in major cities, and they gotta get some scapegoat-ass cop to get on the news and make up shit; lie and say they about to get a handle on the crime. First, it makes for good television, and second, you gotta give the people what they want. And the people wanna believe it ain't gonna never be no more crime, or at the very least, less of it. It makes them sleep good at night just hearing the lies!"

"You think?" Bunny quizzed as she sipped on some more champagne.

"Of course. I don't think, I *know*. And as for that bitch, Tiffany Ross, I knew her. She was a snitch that set dudes up. And between me and you . . ." Dino was trying to prove his dislike for snitches and guys in the game that robbed other cats out in the streets making serious paper and making real bosslike moves just for an easy-ass come up. "As for them bodies that's showing up in that river, niggas can't expect to try to get down on the next money-making motherfucker and not suffer the consequences. You hear me?"

"Really." Bunny started to get in her emotions, knowing where this conversation was headed. It was one thing to bad-mouth Tiffany's bitch ass, but now she knew he was referring to Tariq and her beloved Spoe. Motivated by Dino's basic confession, which was his acknowledgment that he had no problem whatsoever throwing a person into the James River that crossed him, Bunny decided to speed up her plan. Suddenly leaning into his personal space, she nudged her head underneath his chin. Using one hand to play with his well-groomed dreadlocks and the other to massage his growing manhood, Bunny wanted to just bang him really good and get it over with.

Dino's head bobbed backward as he closed his eyes. Lifting her chin with his hand he stuck his tongue deep down her throat. Embraced in passion, he slowly worked his other hand down her curvaceous body, resting it in between her legs. Returning the favor, he now was massaging her moist box. Shoving his hand up in her tight-grip pussy, one finger followed by two worked her over until she was practically screaming out his name. Seeing that she was all in, he swooped her off the couch, carrying her to the king-sized bed. Finding no opposition, he raised her dress up devouring her inners. Hearing her moan, Dino dropped his pants, then went in for the kill. Fucking the dog shit out of her like his life depended on it, he was met with Bunny throwing it back on him. She hadn't had sex since Spoe's death, so she was long overdue to get it in.

Almost forty-five minutes later as they both lay exhausted on the bed, Bunny started to feel guilty. Killing Dino was still very much at the top of her to-do list, but the fact that she'd enjoyed the sex so much was starting to eat away at her conscience. Where a part of her wanted to just get down to business and carry on with the rest of the game plan, the freak in her wanted to maybe go another round or two before sending him on his merry way. Fighting the urge to lower herself to suck his huge dick, she grabbed his hand, urging him to go get in the shower to not only wash some of the sweat off his body, but to also get a special blessing from her. Quick to oblige, Dino jumped up as if he hadn't just put in some serious work and bolted into the bathroom. Turning on the shower, he stepped in underneath the strong flow of hot water, washing his balls as he waited for Bunny to join him.

I can't believe I was all into that nigga sex game like that. I'm so sorry, Spoe; so very sorry. Please forgive me. Don't worry, I'm about to make it right for both me and you. I promise. That ruthless and rotten no-home-training murderer is going to get what he has coming. I love you, Spoe. Talking to herself, Bunny dug into her purse, removing both blades. Holding them tightly, she crept into the steam-filled bathroom. Easily making out Dino's muscular back through the glass door, she felt a strange sense of happiness for what was about to go down. She was seconds away from everything working out the way she planned.

Okay, girl, here we go again! Easing the glass door open, the coldhearted and crazy hood diva stepped her naked body inside. Feeling a slight breeze rush in, Dino knew he was no longer alone in the marble-walled shower. With soap in his eyes and his back still turned, he let Bunny know she was by far one of the most exciting women he'd ever been with, and he hoped to get to know her better in the near future.

Waiting for a verbal response from the female he knew as Krissi, Dino was met with the bitter excruciating pain of not one, but two sharp blades being savagely plunged into his upper torso. Showing no mercy, Bunny brought down one blade overhanded and the other under at a rapid pace, enraged. She repeated the monstrous process until her dreadlocked lover collapsed to his knees. Not saying a word, Dino's lifeless body slumped over underneath the flow of the steaming hot water. Stepping out of the shower to avoid getting his blood even more on her, Bunny allowed him to bleed all the way out until he was well on his way to hell. Bending over his corpse, she cut off one of his dreads as a souvenir. "And, oh yeah, you ho-ass nigga, Spoe said, 'What up!'"

Leaving Dino facedown in the shower, Bunny washed her face along with her kitty cat in the sink and got dressed. *Fuck him! Let them find him when they do!* Placing a do not disturb sign on the door of the Dino's suite, she casually strolled to the elevator, making sure she was not seen. Returning to her own room, which was located several floors below, Bunny pushed the plastic-issued key into key slot of door 217 and entered. Getting comfortable, she took her cell, which was on silent, out of her purse, along with Dino's dread. Immediately she saw she had several missed calls from the same mysterious number and one voice mail. Lying across the bed, Bunny listened to her lone message and couldn't believe her ears.

"This is Detective Chase Dugan of the Richmond Police Department. I was wondering if you could please give me a call at the number showing on your caller identification. I'd like to speak to you in reference to a few important matters that we are investigating. I need for you to please return this call within a twenty-four-hour time span. Once again, this is Detective Chase Dugan of the Richmond Police Department."

Taking her sister's boyfriend's message as more of a direct confirmation sign from God on what she was intending on doing in the first place, Bunny decided to at least call Simone and let her know that her cop beau was sniffing around for answers. "Hey, sis, this is just a heads-up. Your nosy-ass man just called my damn cell, leaving a fucking message. What the fuck you going to do now, bitch?"

"What? What in the world are you talking about? How did he get your phone number?" Simone panicked, and rightfully so.

"Why don't you tell me?" Bunny wasn't about sit

there and be oblivious that Simone may have slipped up somewhere.

"Well, first, what did he say exactly?"

Bunny was even more determined to go ahead with her original game plan and didn't have time to possibly lose her nerve by a long drawn out emotionally charged conversation. "Look, Simone, I don't know what he knows and certainly don't give a shit at this point. I just wanted you to have a heads-up when dealing with him and to tell you I love you, Ginger, and Tallhya's crazy ass. Oh yeah, the rest of my share of the money is in the linen closet. Give it to Ginger's greedy ass! Now, bye, sis, I gotta go."

"Bunny, Bunny . . . Bunny . . ."

Bunny had enough of living life without Spoe. Nothing really mattered to her. She'd taken care of everyone she held responsible for his murder, so now she could rest in peace. Now she could go to sleep for good and wake up in heaven dancing on the clouds with her better half, Spoe. Opening a bottle of pills, she swallowed three handfuls to ensure the deed would be done, washing them down with a bottle of wine she'd brought with her. Making sure her hair was perfect, Bunny Banks lay down in the bed, waiting patiently for death to take her to Spoe.

"Bunny, wait, what are you trying to say? Where are you at? What are you about to do?" Simone didn't receive a reply to any of her questions as she was met with the sound of silence. Bunny had hung up. Trying to call back several times, she repeatedly received the voice mail.

CHAPTER TWENTY-NINE

Simone couldn't believe what was happening. She'd been through so much over the past year that she knew she needed some type of therapy if she ever hoped to be right in the head again. She'd lost her father and become almost destitute. Slapped her stepmother and fought off her father's lecherous business partner. Watched her grandmother collapse at church and die, then lose their family home. Been in a bank robbery and planned another. Taken part in setting up a major drug dealer and fought her mother after taking a gun away from her boyfriend. Watched her sister butcher their own mother and that man. Cut off her mom's hands before dumping their bodies and setting them on fire. She committed her sister Tallhya to a psychiatric facility. Tried to fight her sister's husband and his baby momma in front of the man she was hoping to get closer to. And lastly, got shunned from her childhood church because of some stupid dumb shit she had to be a part of in order to set the wrongs right her grandmother left.

Simone had gone too far to turn back and too far to go on. She felt like she was on the verge of having a serious nervous breakdown. Now after all of that, Bunny had just hung up, having her to believe that she was going to kill herself after saying Chase was snooping around. What else could happen she fretted as her head felt as if it was about to explode. While trying to calm her nerves, there was a knock at the door. Praying it was Bunny saying she was playing some sort of cruel, twisted joke, Simone flung the door wide open. Unfortunately, it wasn't Bunny but two policemen.

"Yes, Officers. How can I help you?"

"Ma'am, are you the family of a Mr. Gene Banks?" Their expressions were solemn as they both looked her in the face.

Simone was in a panicked state as she answered, "Yes, yes, I am. I'm his sister. What's wrong with my brother? What's going on?"

The policeman had made these types of house calls before and hated doing so. "Well, it seems he was involved in some kind of what we think was a hate crime. He and several other openly gay men were beaten to death near the park. We need for you to come down to the morgue and possibly identify his body. This is the address listed on his driver's license."

Simone's mouth dropped open. She couldn't speak, and her feet couldn't move. As the room started to spin and she grew increasingly dizzy, the last thing she remembered before blacking out was Chase's voice asking the two officers what they were doing at the house. When she finally came to, she was lying on the couch and Chase was wiping her face with a wet rag he'd gotten out of the linen closet.

"Hey, Chase, did I hear . . ."

Before she could finish asking the question, he answered for her. "Yes, Simone, it was bad news about your brother. He's dead; killed by some idiots."

Simone started sobbing in his arms. "Oh, Chase, not my brother too. It can't be! Why?"

"Simone, I don't know what to say."

"Damn, Chase, I love you so much. My life is so crazy. I wish Ginger was still alive and things were different! I wish I could just turn back the hands of time. If we could just go somewhere and be together . . . just you and me, life would be perfect." Her tears wet his shirt as he grew confused on what to do next. He loved her too and was torn considering he knew there was a direct link with Bunny and the criminal cases he was investigating.

When Simone blurted out that the doctors thought she had cancer and she hoped he wouldn't abandon her, Detective Chase Dugan knew against his better judgment what he had to do . . . forget he'd found the bag of stolen money from the bank robbery he'd discovered in the linen closet and take care of the woman he loved—even if it cost him his badge. At the end of the day, love was all that truly mattered to him. Hopefully, he'd never find out all the Banks sisters' deep dark secrets, because who knows if love for anyone is really that strong!

ORDER FORM
URBAN BOOKS, LLC
97 N. 18th Street
Wyandanch, NY 11798

Name (please print):_____

Address: _____

City/State: _____

Zip: _____

QTY	TITLES	PRICE

Shipping and handling-add $3.50 for 1st book, then $1.75 for each additional book.
Please send a check payable to:
     Urban Books, LLC
Please allow 4–6 weeks for delivery